DANGEROUS GROUND

Yeah, it's complicated...

Special Agents for the Department of Diplomatic Security, Taylor MacAllister and Will Brandt have been partners and best friends for three years, but everything changed the night Taylor admitted the truth about his feelings for Will. But it's complicated...

Taylor agreed to a camping trip in the High Sierras—despite the fact that he hates camping—because Will wants a chance to save their partnership. But the trip is a disaster from the first, and things rapidly go from bad to worse when they find a crashed plane and a couple of million dollars in stolen money.

With a trio of murderous robbers trailing them, Will and Taylor are on dangerous ground, fighting for their partnership, their passion...and their lives.

DANGEROUS GROUND

JOSH LANYON

VELLICHOR BOOKS
An imprint of JustJoshin Publishing, Inc.

DANGEROUS GROUND
January 2020

Cover by Ron Perry for Ron Perry Graphic Design
Book design by Kevin Burton Smith
Edited by Judith David & Keren Reed

Published in the United States of America

JustJoshin Publishing, Inc.
3053 Rancho Vista Blvd.
Suite 116
Palmdale, CA 93551
www.joshlanyon.com

CHAPTER ONE

The nose of the red and white twin engine Baron 58 was crunched deep into the bottom of the wooded ravine. Mud and debris covered the cockpit windows. One wing had been sheared off when the plane crashed through the surrounding pines, knocking three of them over. The other wing was partially buckled beneath the craft. The tail of the plane had broken off and lay several yards down the ravine.

Taylor mopped his face on the flannel sleeve of his shirt. Ten thousand feet up in the High Sierras, the sun was still plenty warm despite the chill spring air.

Behind him, Will said, "Either the pilot was unfamiliar with the terrain or he didn't have a lot of experience with mountain flying. Out here, avoiding box canyons is one of the first things you learn."

"Take a look at this," Taylor said, and Will made his way to him across the rocky, uneven slope. Taylor pointed to the fuselage. "You see those registration numbers?"

"N81BH." Will's blue eyes met Taylor's. "Now why does that sound so familiar?"

Taylor grinned. "It's the plane used in that Tahoe casino heist last year."

Will whistled, long and low.

"Yeah," agreed Taylor. Just for a moment he let his gaze linger on the other man's lean, square-jawed features. Will's hair, brown and shining in the sun, fell boyishly into his eyes. He hadn't shaved in three days, and the dark stubble gave him a rugged, sexy look—very different from the normal nine to five Will. Not that they exactly worked nine to five at the Bureau of Diplomatic Security.

Will's gaze held his for a moment, and Taylor looked away, focusing on the plane's registration numbers again.

"What'd they get away with again?" Will asked in a making conversation kind of voice. "Something in the neighborhood of 2.3 million, was it?"

"That and murder," Taylor said grimly. "They shot two sheriff's deputies making their getaway." These days he was touchy about law enforcement officers getting gunned down.

"Doesn't look like they got away far." Will moved toward the open door of the plane. He hopped lightly up onto the broken wing, and for a moment Taylor felt a twinge of envy. He was still moving slowly after his own shooting six weeks ago; sometimes he felt like he was never going to get it all back: the strength, the speed—the confidence—he had always taken for granted. He felt old at thirty-one.

He walked toward the broken off tail piece, and Will—only half-joking—called, "Watch out for snakes, MacAllister."

"You had to say that, didn't you, Brandt?" Taylor threw back. He studied the rim of the ravine. It had been winter when three masked men with automatic weapons robbed the Black Wolf Casino on the Nevada border of Lake Tahoe. They had fled to the nearby airport, hijacked a plane, and disappeared into the snowy December night.

Local law enforcement had theorized the Beechcraft Baron crashed in the High Sierras, but the weather and the terrain had inhibited searchers. It was clear to Taylor now that even under the best conditions, it would have been just about impossible to spot the little plane tucked away in the crevice of this mountainside.

He glanced back, but Will had vanished inside the wrecked plane. He could hear the eerie creak and groan of the aircraft as Will moved around inside.

Taylor worked his way around the crash site. Not their area of expertise, of course, but he knew what to look for.

Scattered engine parts and broken glass were strewn everywhere. A couple of seats had been thrown clear and were relatively intact. There was a weathered plank of wood that must have originally been a table or a desk, and some broken light fixtures and vinyl parts of storage bins. The plane could have carried five passengers in addition to the pilot. The casino had been hit by three bandits; the fourth had been driving the getaway car that sped them to Truckee Tahoe Airport. Four people would have inevitably left DNA evidence, but the crash site was four months old and contaminated by the elements and wildlife. He glanced around at the sound of Will's boots on the loose rock.

Will said, "The pilot's inside. No one else."

That was no surprise. The initial investigation had cleared the pilot of involvement in the robbery; if he'd been alive, he would have contacted the authorities. Taylor thought it over. "No sign there were any passengers on board when she went down."

"What about an incriminating black tie?" Will referred to the famous narrow black necktie that legendary hijacker D.B. Cooper left on the Boeing 727 he jumped out of way back in 1971.

"Not so much as a stray sock."

"Then I guess they weren't doing laundry up there," Will remarked, and Taylor drew a blank.

"You know how one sock always gets lost—forget it." It was a lame joke, but once Taylor would have known instantly what Will meant. Once Taylor would have laughed. "Parachutes?" Will asked.

"No parachutes."

"None?"

"Doesn't look like it," Taylor said.

"Interesting. The pilot's got a bullet through his skull."

"Ah," said Taylor.

"Yep."

Their eyes met.

"Come take a look," Will invited, and Taylor followed him back to the front section of the plane.

Will sprang onto the wing, reaching a hand down for Taylor, and with a grimace, Taylor accepted his help, vaulting up beside him. The wing bobbed beneath their weight, and Will steadied him, hands on Taylor's waist for an instant.

Taylor moved away. Not that he minded Will's hands on him—there was nothing he'd have liked more than Will's hands on him—but this had nothing to do with attraction and everything to do with lack of confidence. A lack of confidence in Taylor being able to look after himself. Not that Will had said so, but it was clear to Taylor—and maybe it was clear to Will too, which might explain what the hell they were doing up in the High Sierras one week before Taylor was officially due to start back at work.

Because if they couldn't figure this out—get past it—they were through as a team. Regardless of the fact that so far no one had admitted there was even a problem.

"After you," Will said, waving him into the gloomy and rotting interior of the plane with exaggerated courtesy. Taylor gave him a wry smile and ducked inside.

"Jesus. Something's made itself right at home in here."

"Yeah. Maybe a marmot. Or a weasel. Something relatively small." Will's breath was warm against the back of Taylor's neck.

"Relatively small is good," Taylor muttered, and Will laughed.

"Unless it's a skunk."

Almost four years they'd been together: partners and friends—good friends—but maybe that was over now. Taylor didn't want to think so, but —

His boot turned on a broken door lever, and Will's hand shot out, steadying him. Taylor pulled away, just managing to control his impatience.

Yeah, that was the problem. Will didn't think Taylor was capable of taking two steps without Will there to keep an eye on him.

And that was guilt. Pure and simple. Not friendship, not one partner watching another partner's back, not even the normal overprotectiveness of one partner for his injured-in-the-line-of-duty opposite number. No, this was guilt because of the way Taylor felt about Will—because Will didn't feel the same. And somehow Will had managed to convince himself that that was part of the reason Taylor had stopped a bullet.

He clambered across the empty copilot's seat and studied the remains of the dead pilot slumped over the instrument dashboard control panel. The pilot's clothes were in rags, deteriorated and torn. Bacteria, insects, and animals had reduced the body to a mostly skeletal state. Not entirely skeletal, unfortunately, but Taylor had seen worse as a special agent posted in Afghanistan. He examined the corpse dispassionately, noting position, even while recognizing that animals had been at it. Some of the smaller bones of the hands and feet were missing.

"One bullet to the back of the head," he said.

"Yep," Will replied. "While the plane was still in flight."

Taylor glanced down at the jammed throttle. "And then the hijackers bailed out," he agreed. This part at least still worked between them. They still could work a crime scene with that single-mindedness that had earned the attention and approval of their superiors.

Not that they investigated many homicides at the Bureau of Diplomatic Security. Mostly they helped in the extradition of fugitives who fled the country, or ran interference for local law enforcement agencies with foreign police departments. But now and then they got to...get their feet wet. Some times were a little wetter than others. Taylor rubbed his chest absently.

"In the middle of the night and in the middle of nowhere," Will said. "Hard to believe all four of them made it out of these mountains safely. FBI and the local law were all over these woods within twenty-four hours."

"Yeah, but it was snowing, remember."

"Those guys are trained."

"They missed the plane."

"The plane wasn't making for the main highway."

"Maybe the bad guys were local," Taylor said. "Maybe they knew the terrain."

"Wasn't the prevailing theory, was it?"

"No." He backed out of the cockpit, and Will did it again—rested his hand on Taylor's back to stabilize him—although Taylor's balance was fine, physically and emotionally.

He gritted his jaw, biting back anything that would widen the rift between them. Will's friendship was better than nothing, right? And there had been a brief and truly hellish period when he thought he'd lost that, so…shut up and be grateful, yeah?

Yeah.

Will jumped down to the ground and reached up a hand. Taylor ignored the hand, and dropped down beside him—which jarred his rib cage and hurt like fuck. He did his best to hide the fact.

"More likely what's left of 'em is scattered through these woods," Will commented, and Taylor grimaced.

"There's a thought."

"Imagine jumping out of a plane into freezing rain and whatever that headwind was? Eighteen knots. Maybe more."

"Maybe someone was waiting for them on the ground."

Will nodded thoughtfully. "Two and an almost-half million divides nicely between five."

Taylor grunted. Didn't it just? Kneeling by his pack, he unzipped it, dug through his clothes and supplies, searching for something on which he could note the crash site coordinates. It was sheer luck they'd stumbled on it this time. He found the small notebook he'd tossed in, fished further and found a pen, pulling the cap off with his teeth. He squinted up at the anvil-shaped cliff to the right of the canyon. The sun was starting to sink in the sky. He rose.

Will moved next to him, looking over his shoulder, and just that much proximity unsettled Taylor. It took effort not to move away, turn his back. Will smelled like sunshine and flannel and his own clean sweat as he brushed against Taylor's arm, frowning down at Taylor's diagram.

"What's that supposed to be? A chafing dish?"

Taylor pointed the pen. "It's that…thing. Dome or whatever you call it."

"If you say so, Picasso." Will unfolded his map. "Let me borrow your pen."

Taylor handed his pen over, and Will circled a spot on the map, before folding it up again, and shoving it in the back pocket of his desert camo pants.

"Well, hell," he said, "I guess we should start back down, notify the authorities we found their missing aircraft."

Will looked at him inquiringly, and Taylor nodded. That was the logical thing to do, after all. But he wasn't happy about it. Three days into their "vacation" they weren't any closer to bridging the distance yawning between them—and it would be a long time before they had this kind of opportunity again. By then it might be too late. Whereas this plane had been sitting here for over four months; would another four days really make a difference?

"Right. We'll rest up tonight and head back tomorrow then," Will added, after a moment.

Taylor directed a narrow look his way, but the truth was he *was* fatigued, and climbing in the dark would have been stupid even if he wasn't. So he nodded again, curtly, and tossed the notebook and diagram back into his pack.

* * * * *

Will was tired. Pleasantly tired. Taylor was exhausted. Not that he'd admit it, but Will could tell by the way he dropped down by the campfire while Will finished pitching their two-man tent.

One eye on Taylor, Will stowed their sleeping bags inside the Eureka Apex XT. He pulled Taylor's Therm-a-Rest sleeping pad out of his own backpack where he'd managed to stash it that morning without Taylor noticing, and spread it out on the floor of the tent. He opened the valve and left the pad inflating while he went to join Taylor at the fire.

"Hungry?"

"Always." Taylor's grin was wry—and so was Will's meeting it. Taylor ate like a horse—even in the hospital—although where he put it was anyone's guess. He was all whippy muscle and fine bones that seemed to be made out of titanium. It was easy to look at him and dismiss him as a threat, but anyone who'd ever tangled with him didn't make that mistake twice.

He was too thin now, though, which was why Will was carrying about three pounds more food in his pack than they probably needed. He watched Taylor feeding wood into the flames. In the firelight his face was all sharps and angles. His eyes looked almost black with fatigue—they weren't black, though, they were a kind of burnished green—an indefinable shade of bronze that reminded Will of old armor. Very striking with his black hair—Will's gaze lingered on Taylor's hair, on that odd single streak of silver since the shooting.

He didn't want to think about the shooting. Didn't want to think about finding Taylor in a dingy storeroom with his shirt and blazer soaked in blood—Taylor struggling for each anguished breath. He still had nightmares about that.

He said, talking himself away from the memory, "Well, monsieur, tonight zee specials are zee beef stroganoff, zee Mexican-style chicken, or zee lasagna with meat sauce."

"What won't they freeze-dry next?" Taylor marveled.

"Nothing. You name it, they'll freeze-dry it. We've got Neapolitan ice cream for dessert."

"You're kidding."

"Just like the astronauts eat."

"We pay astronauts to sit around drinking Tang and eating freeze-dried ice cream?"

"Your tax dollars at work." Will's eyes assessed Taylor. "Here." He shifted, pulled his flask out of his hip pocket, unscrewed the cap, and handed it to Taylor. "Before dinner cocktails."

"Cheers." Taylor took a swig and shuddered.

"Hey," Will protested. "That's Sam Houston bourbon. You know how hard that it is to find?"

"Yeah, I know. I bought you a bottle for Christmas year before last."

"That's right. Then you know just how good this is."

"Not if you don't like it." But Taylor was smiling—which was good to see. Not too many smiles between them since that last night at Will's house. And he wanted to think about that even less than he wanted to think about Taylor getting shot.

"Son, that bourbon will put hair on your chest," he said.

"Yeah, well, unlike you I prefer my bears in the woods."

There was a brief uncomfortable pause while they both remembered a certain naval officer, and then Taylor took another swig and handed the flask back to Will.

"Thanks."

Will grunted acknowledgment.

He thought about telling Taylor he hadn't seen Bradley since that god-awful night, but that was liable to make things worse—it would certainly confuse the issue, because regardless of what Taylor believed, the issue had never been Lieutenant Commander David Bradley.

Taylor put a hand to the small of his back, arching a little, wincing—and Will watched him, chewing the inside of his cheek, thinking it over. It was taking a while to get back into sync, that was all. It was just going to take a little time. Sure, Taylor was moody, a little distant, but he still wasn't 100 percent.

He was getting there, though. Getting there fast—because once Taylor put his mind to a thing, it was as good as done. Usually. When he started back at work he'd be stuck on desk duty for a couple of weeks, maybe even a month or so, but he'd be back in the field before long, and Will was counting the days. He missed Taylor like he'd miss his right arm. Maybe more.

Even now he was afraid—but there was no point thinking like that. They were okay. They just needed time to work through it. And the best way to do that was to leave the past alone.

"Warm enough?" he asked.

Taylor gave him a long, unfriendly look.

"Hey, just asking." Will rose. "I was going to get a sweater out of my bag for myself."

Taylor relaxed. "Yeah. Can you grab my fleece vest?"

Will nodded, and passing Taylor, took a swipe at the back of his head, which Taylor neatly ducked.

* * * * *

They had instant black bean soup and the Mexican-style chicken for dinner, and followed it up with the freeze-dried ice cream and coffee.

"It's not bad," Taylor offered, breaking off a piece of ice cream and popping it into his mouth.

Actually the ice cream wasn't that bad. It crunched when you put it into your mouth, then dissolved immediately, but Will said, "What do you know? You'll eat anything. If I didn't watch out you'd be eating poison mushrooms or poison berries or poison oak."

Taylor grinned. It was true; he was a city boy through and through. Will was the outdoors guy. He was the one who thought a week of camping and hiking was what they needed to get back on track; Taylor was humoring him by coming along on this trip. In fact, Will was still a little surprised Taylor had agreed. Taylor's idea of vacation time well spent was on the water and in the sun: renting a house boat—like they had last summer—or deep sea fishing—which Taylor had done on his own the year before.

"They never did arrest anyone in connection with that heist, did they?" Taylor said thoughtfully, after a few more minutes of companionable chewing.

"What heist?"

Taylor threw him an impatient look. "The robbery at the Black Wolf Casino."

"Oh. Not that I heard. I wasn't really following it." Taylor had a brain like a computer when it came to crimes and unsolved mysteries. When Will wasn't working, which, granted, was rarely, the last thing he wanted to do was think about crooks and crime—especially the ones that had nothing to do with them.

But Taylor was shaking his head like Will was truly a lost cause, so he volunteered, "There was something about the croupier, right? She was questioned a couple of times."

"Yeah. Questioned but never charged." He shivered.

Will frowned. "You all right?"

"*Jesus*, Brandt, will you give it a fucking *rest*!" And just like that, Taylor was unsmiling, stone-faced and hostile.

There was a short, sharp silence. "Christ, you can be an unpleasant bastard," Will said finally, evenly. He threw the last of his foil-wrapped ice cream into the fire, and the flames jumped, sparks shooting up with bits of blackened metal.

Taylor said tersely, "You want a more pleasant bastard for a partner, say the word."

The instant aggression caught Will off guard. Where the hell had it come from? "No, I don't want someone more pleasant," he said. "I don't want a new partner."

Taylor stared at the fire. "Maybe I do," he said quietly.

Will stared at him. He felt like he'd been sucker punched. Dopey and...off-kilter.

"Why'd you say that?" he asked finally into the raw silence between them.

He saw Taylor's throat move, saw him swallowing hard, and he understood that although Taylor had spoken on impulse, he meant it—and that he was absorbing that truth even as Will was.

"We're good together," Will said, not giving Taylor time to answer—afraid that if Taylor put it into words they wouldn't be able to go back from it. "We're...the best. Partners and friends."

He realized he was gripping his coffee cup so hard he was about to snap the plastic handle.

Taylor said, his voice low but steady, "Yeah. We are. But...it might be better for both of us if we were reteamed."

"Better for you, you mean?"

Taylor met his eyes. "Yeah. Better for me."

And now Will was getting angry. It took him a moment to recognize the symptoms because he wasn't a guy who got mad easily or often—and never at Taylor. Exasperated, maybe. Disapproving sometimes, yeah. But angry? Not with Taylor. Not even for getting himself shot like a goddamned wet-behind-the-ears recruit. But that prickling flush beneath his skin, that pounding in his temples, that rush of adrenaline—that was anger. And it was all for Taylor.

Will threw his cup away and stood up—aware that Taylor tensed. Which made him even madder—and Will was plenty mad already. "Oh, I get it," he said. "This is payback. This is you getting your own back—holding the partnership hostage to your hurt ego. This is all because I won't sleep with you, isn't it? That's what it's really about."

And Taylor said in that same infuriatingly even tone, "If that's what you want to think, go ahead."

Right. Taylor—the guy who jumped first and thought second, if at all; who couldn't stop shooting his mouth off if his life depended on it; who thought three months equaled the love of a lifetime—

suddenly *he* was Mr. Cool and Reasonable. What a goddamn laugh. Mr. Wounded Dignity sitting there staring at Will with those wide, bleak eyes.

"What am I supposed to think?" Will asked, and it took effort to keep his voice as level as Taylor's. "That you're in love? We both know what this is about, and it ain't love, buddy boy. You just can't handle the fact that anyone could turn you down."

"Fuck you," Taylor said, abandoning the cool and reasonable thing.

"My point exactly," Will shot back. "And you know what? Fine. If that's what I have to do to hold this team together, fine. Let's fuck. Let's get it out of the way once and for all. If that's your price, then okay. I'm more than willing to take one for the team—or am I supposed to do you? Whichever is fine by me because unlike you, MacAllister, I —"

With an inarticulate sound, Taylor launched himself at Will, and Will, unprepared, fell back over the log he'd been sitting on, head ringing from Taylor's fist connecting with his jaw. This was rage, not passion, although for one bewildered instant Will's body processed the feel of Taylor's hard, thin, muscular length landing on top of his own body as a good thing—a very good thing.

This was followed by the very bad thing of Taylor trying to knee him in the guts—which sent a new and clearer message to Will's mind and body.

And there was nothing Will would have loved more than to let go and pulverize Taylor, to take him apart, piece by piece, but he didn't forget for an instant—even if Taylor did—how physically vulnerable Taylor still was; so his efforts went into keeping Taylor from injuring himself—which was not easy to do wriggling and rolling around on the uneven ground. Even at 75 percent, Taylor was a significant threat, and Will took a few hits before he managed to wind his arms around the other man's torso, yanking him into a sitting position facing Will, and immobilizing him in a butterfly lock.

Taylor tried a couple of heaves, but he had tired fast. Will was the better wrestler anyway, being taller, broader, and heavier. Taylor relied on speed and surprise; he went in for all kinds of esoteric martial arts, which was fine unless someone like Will got him on the ground. Taylor was usually too smart to let that happen, which just went to show how furious he was.

Will could feel that fury still shaking Taylor—locked in this ugly parody of a lover's embrace. He shook with exhaustion too, breath shuddering in his lungs as he panted into Will's shoulder. His wind was shit these days, his heart banging frantically against Will's. These marks of physical distress undermined Will's own anger, reminding him how recently he had almost lost Taylor for good.

Taylor's moist breath against Will's ear was sending a confusingly erotic message, his body hot and sweaty—but Christ, he was thin. Will could feel—could practically count—ribs, the hard links of spine, the ridges of scapula in Taylor's fleshless back. And it scared him; his hold changed instinctively from lock to hug.

"You crazy bastard," he muttered into Taylor's hair.

Taylor struggled again, and this time Will let him go. Taylor got up, not looking at Will, not speaking, walking unsteadily, but with a peculiar dignity, over to the tent.

Watching him, Will opened his mouth, then shut it. Why the hell would he apologize? Taylor had jumped *him.* He watched, scowling, as Taylor crawled inside the tent, rolled out his sleeping bag onto the air mattress Will had remembered to set up for him, pulled his boots off, and climbed into the bag, pulling the flap over his head—like something going back into its shell.

This is stupid, Will thought. We neither of us want this. But what he said was, "Sweet dreams to you too."

Taylor said nothing.

CHAPTER TWO

Will looked like hell. Eyes red-rimmed, hair ruffled. There was a black-and-blue bruise on his jaw, which Taylor tried to feel sorry about—but Will looked sorry enough for himself for both of them.

Taylor watched him pour a shot of bourbon into his coffee without comment. Yep, Will was definitely having a bad day, and it was only seven o'clock in the morning.

As though reading his thoughts, Will looked up and met his eyes. Taylor, feeling weirdly self-conscious, looked away.

"So I guess we're still not speaking this morning?" Will asked.

And despite the fact that he didn't want to fight with Will, that he wanted to find some way to step back from the precipice he teetered on, Taylor shrugged and said coolly, "What did you want to talk about?"

And Will just gave a kind of disgusted half-laugh, and turned back to his spiked coffee.

So that was that.

They moved around camp, neither of them speaking, moving efficiently and swiftly as they breakfasted and then packed up—like the day before and the day before that, only this morning the silence between them was not the easy silence of a long and comfortable partnership; it was as heavy and ominous as the rain clouds to the north.

It was still early in the season—and the weather poor enough—that they met no one as they started down the steep trail, stepping carefully on the gravel and small stones. It was a strenuous descent, requiring attention, and Taylor was glad to concentrate on something besides Will. He'd been thinking about Will way too much lately. For the last year, really.

The view was spectacular: huge clouds rolling in from the north, snow-covered mountains all around them, and a long, green valley way below, moody sunlight glinting off the surface of a slate blue lake. The scent of sagebrush was in the air—and the hum of bees. The sun felt good on his face after weeks of being indoors in bed.

Will, the experienced hiker, went first down the trail. The set of his wide shoulders was uncompromising, his back ramrod straight as though he could feel Taylor's stare resting between his shoulder blades—which he probably could. They'd got pretty good at reading each other's thoughts, and half the time they communicated with no more than a glance.

Back when they used to communicate.

The bulky sweater and comfortable fatigues couldn't conceal the lithe beauty of that tall, strong male body. Will was the most naturally gorgeous guy Taylor had ever known. And no little part of his attractiveness had to do with the fact that he was pretty much unaware of just how good-looking he was. Taylor's gaze dropped automatically to Will's taut ass. Yep, gorgeous.

Will's boot slipped on shale, and Taylor's hand shot out, grabbing him, steadying him.

Will grunted thanks, not looking at him. Taylor let go reluctantly.

It was weird the way his body craved contact with Will's. Any contact. A nudge in the ribs or a pat on the ass. It was like an addiction. In the hospital he'd lived every day waiting for Will to drop by—and to give Will credit, he'd managed to visit almost every single day, even if it was just for a few minutes. It had been strange, though, with Will so gentle and careful with him; at the time Taylor had been too ill to question it.

Even when Will didn't touch him, when he just stood next to him, Taylor could feel his nearness in every cell, his skin anticipating Will's touch—longing for the lover's touch that never came. Was *never* going to come, because Will didn't feel that way about him.

They couldn't go on like this. Even Will had to see that—although Will was pretty good at not seeing what he didn't want to see.

They stopped midmorning for water and granola bars, still not looking at each other, still not talking. Will consulted his map. Checked his compass. High overhead, a pair of golden eagles threw insults at each other.

"Are they mating?" Taylor asked, suddenly tired of the stand off. He missed Will, missed their old companionship. He'd been missing him for six weeks—and he was liable to be missing him from now on. It seemed worth making an effort for whatever was left of their trip.

Will glanced skyward briefly. His eyes were very blue in his tanned face. They held Taylor's gaze gravely. "That's your idea of romance?"

He was partly kidding, but partly not, and Taylor felt himself coloring.

"Hey." He lifted a shoulder. Not exactly sparkling repartee, but he didn't want to fight anymore, didn't know what Will wanted. He couldn't not feel what he felt; he'd tried that—had tried for well over a year to talk himself out of feeling what was obviously unwanted and unwelcome.

Will snorted, but he was smiling. Sort of. "You're a nut, MacAllister. Did I ever tell you that?"

"A girl never gets tired of hearing it," Taylor deadpanned, and Will did laugh then. He shoved the map back into his pocket, shrugged on his backpack.

* * * * *

They reached the meadow a little after one o'clock. The clouds roiling overhead were thunderous and black. The pine and fir trees were singing and swaying in the wind; the lake was choppy and dark. The gray green grass rippled like the earth was breathing beneath their feet.

"Let's get under the trees," Will said. "We'll pitch the tent and have lunch. Wait it out."

Taylor could see he was worried about the worsening weather conditions; Taylor was just grateful for flat terrain. He'd wanted to call for a rest an hour earlier, but he'd have died first. He could feel the ache of coming rain in his chest, and told himself to get used to it. The doctors had said the broken ribs were going to hurt forever—especially when it rained. The bullet had torn through skin, muscles, and a couple of ribs. Following the shock of impact—like a land mine going off inside his chest—the pain had been unbelievable. Unimaginable.

The miracle had been that no major blood vessels had been hit while the bullet ricocheted around his chest cavity. But it hadn't felt like a miracle at the time. His right lung had begun to squeeze, he'd had to struggle for each short breath, and it had been agony—like getting stabbed over and over. His vision had grayed out, he hadn't been able to call out or move, feeling the warm spill of his own blood on his chilled skin—and the blood had felt good, that's how cold he'd been. Cold to the core.

And then Will had been there. And he'd been glad. Glad for the chance to see him one last time, to say good-bye, even if it was just inside his own head because he sure wasn't capable of speech. And the expression on Will's face had been comforting. At least at the time. Now he knew it for what it was. Guilt. But at the time it had looked like something else, something it had been worth dying to see.

He glanced at Will, walking beside him as they tramped across the long meadow. Will appeared a million miles away, but he felt Taylor's gaze and looked over at him. He opened his mouth, and then closed it, and Taylor knew he had been about to ask if Taylor was all right.

And as tired as he was of Will asking if he was okay, he realized he preferred that to this new awkwardness. And he sure as hell preferred it to Will no longer giving a damn.

He started to say so, but something in the brush caught his attention: the sheen of black material.

"Hey," he said, stopping and nodding.

Will glanced at him, tracked his gaze, and saw exactly what Taylor had. He followed as Taylor waded into the currant bushes dragging what at first glance appeared to be a black seat cushion from out of the bush.

"It's a parachute," Will said, taking it from Taylor and turning it over.

Taylor nodded. "Still packed."

They met each other's gaze, and Taylor raised an eyebrow.

"Let's have a little look-see," Will drawled.

"I'll take the right."

They separated, fanning out across the meadow. It took less than half an hour to locate the other three parachutes—two still packed, one torn wide open by something with claws and a lot of optimism. It seemed clear to Taylor that all four parachutes had been jettisoned at the same time. The speed of the plane and the headwind had resulted in several yards between each landing, but not nearly the distance which would have resulted from dropping them out the plane door at deliberate intervals.

"That's it," Taylor said as Will rejoined him. "The fifth chute will have gone with the hijacker."

"Then it won't have gone far." Will's face was grim. He was staring past Taylor, and Taylor turned. Near the lake the trees grew in a thick wall of white firs, Jeffrey pines, and incense cedars. And there, dangling from a twenty-feet tall cedar like a dreadful Christmas tree ornament, was what remained of the missing parachutist.

* * * * *

"He's carrying a knapsack," Taylor commented, as they stood gazing up at the macabre thing swinging gently in the wind.

"Christ," Will said.

"I'll go up." Taylor started forward, but Will caught his arm.

"Uh, no, you sure won't."

That of course was a big mistake; Taylor freed himself, his face hard again. "Is that so?"

Will said calmly, "Yep, MacAllister, that is so." Even if he had to knock Taylor on his ass to make it so.

"I'm lighter, I'm faster —"

"You're sure as hell not faster these days."

Which was true, but not guaranteed to win points. But Will wasn't interested in winning points; he was interested in keeping Taylor in one piece, whatever it took, and maybe Taylor read that resolve in Will's eyes because after a pause, he shrugged. Said tersely, "Hey, suit yourself. You always do."

The injustice of that stung, and although Will had told himself he was not going to lose his temper again, that he could be patient, that Taylor and their partnership was worth working this through—whatever the hell *this* was and however much work it took—all the same he bit right back, "Christ, that's rich coming from *you*."

And instantly Taylor was cool, his body deceptively relaxed—a fighter poised for action. Oh, yes, Will had seen that loose, easy stance a hundred times. "What's that supposed to mean?"

"Forget it."

Taylor got in front of him. "I don't want to forget it."

Un-fucking-believable. In fact, if he didn't know better he'd have suspected Taylor had been shot in his goddamn head. Who was this stranger who had taken over Taylor's body?

Will planted both hands on Taylor's chest and pushed him back a step. "What, are we supposed to have another wrestling match now?"

The physical aggression caught Taylor off guard, and Will pressed his advantage. "You're self-centered, MacAllister. You do whatever you want whenever you feel like it, and to hell with everybody else. This is a perfect example."

"This?" Another time and place Taylor's indignation might have been funny. "I didn't even want to come on this goddamned trip. I did it for you. And what the hell you wanted out of it beats me since you obviously —" He broke off, and to their mutual horror, for an instant appeared to be choked with emotion.

Anger, Will could deal with. Arrogance, aggression, he knew what to do. This? No.

Before he had time to rethink, he reached out—and just in time stopped himself from pulling Taylor into his arms. He settled for squeezing those rigid shoulders. "Look, Taylor, all I meant was…you don't always think things through." He offered a tentative smile. "Come on, I've known you three years. We both know your track record. When it comes to relationships you think with your dick and damn the torpedoes. And yes, for the record, I…find you attractive too. You know that. But there's more at stake here. I don't want to screw up our friendship or our partnership because we sleep together."

"Why would it screw anything up?" Taylor was looking at him so seriously. So…earnestly. It cut him up inside. The last thing he wanted to do was hurt Taylor. Ever. But Taylor just wouldn't stay down. He kept getting up and coming back for more. And what the hell was Will supposed to do?

He said, struggling for patience, "It's already screwing everything up and we haven't even done it!"

"Why couldn't we give it a real shot?"

"What are you talking about? Give it a real shot? Give *what* a real shot?" Will let go of him, and gestured to the scene before them. "Here's why. Because we're in the middle of a crime scene and we're arguing about our goddamned *romance*."

He couldn't stand the look on Taylor's face, so he turned away. What they needed was a climbing harness but…what the hell. He jumped for the lowest limb, wrapped his legs partway around the thick trunk, and hauled himself up a couple of feet. Blowing out, he reached up for the next branch. He swung himself up, stretched for another tree limb—and began to climb.

At first it was like crawling through undergrowth, but then the branches spread out, and he was able to see what he was doing and move more freely. He had a good head for heights, and the tree had thick, dark, irregular bark, making it easier for his boots to find purchase. The limbs were plentiful. Yellow cones rained down as he swarmed up through the cinnamon-scented branches.

The tree groaned, swaying in the wind. Will looked up, and the feet of the dead parachutist were hanging an arm's length away.

Pausing to pull the knife from his ankle sheath, he looked down, surprised to see how small and faraway Taylor looked.

"Lightning to the north," Taylor called, batting away another hurtling cone. And then… "Brandt—maybe this wasn't such a good idea."

"Now you tell me," Will muttered. He called back, "Simmer down, buddy boy. It's under control."

Knife in hand, he studied the tangle of parachute and parachutist. Wind and weather had reduced the chute to ribbons, and the body wasn't in much better shape. A tree limb thrust from the hijacker's waist like a spear; he must have been impaled as he crashed through the branches. Crime really didn't pay.

His own position wasn't quite right…

Will transferred the knife to his mouth, and edged around the trunk, feeling cautiously for footholds. It was hard to see... He pulled himself up to another branch, balancing, and edged closer to the sack of rotting clothes, flesh, and bones.

And all the fresh pine scent in the world wasn't helping...

"That is definitely lightning," Taylor said from below. He had that irritable sound he got when he was nervous. "You mind not taking all day, Brandt?"

"Yeah, I mind. It's my vacation; I'll spend it any damn way I please."

"Asshole." But he could hear the unwilling laugh in Taylor's voice.

Will steeled himself and felt over the dead man's rags, seeking a wallet or any kind of identification. He didn't expect to find any, and he wasn't disappointed. That done, he began to saw with his free hand at the straps of the knapsack. He tried to be careful, but he was in a hurry now, and the clothes and corpse began to come apart with his tugging. One of the black boots fell.

Fuck. *Fuck.* He wiped his face on his shoulder. Called down, "Stand back, MacAllister. It's raining men."

"Are you *kidding* me?"

His tone was priceless. Will bit back a ferocious grin, and went back to hacking at the knapsack straps. A few more slices and he had it. The backpack tumbled down a few feet, knocking needles and cones and twigs loose—along with the corpse's other boot.

Will lowered himself down swiftly, pursuing the knapsack. He found it lodged in the V of the trunk and a branch.

Grabbing it by the severed straps, he swung it once, twice, out beyond the span of the branches—and let it fly. "MacAllister, heads up!"

The pack went sailing and then dropped to earth like a stone.

Will let himself down fast, ignoring the scrape of rough bark on his hands. A few feet from the ground he balanced on a thick limb.

Taylor had retrieved the bag. He knelt in the mud and pine needles, knapsack wide open, staring up at Will. “You sure you don’t want to run away to Mexico with me?” He held up a neatly bound stack of greenbacks.

“Nah.” Will jumped down, landing lightly on the soft wet earth. “Salsa gives you indigestion.”

“True.” Taylor tossed the stack of dollars to Will.

The money felt damp, sinister to his touch. He thumbed through it. Benjamin Franklin’s skeptical expression flashed by over and over.

The rain began to fall.

CHAPTER THREE

"You warm enough?"

Taylor didn't bother to respond, staring out the mesh window of the tent at the rain sheeting down the sides.

Of course he was cold. He was freezing his ass off. Will had told him not to wear Levi's. He'd told him to dress in layers. Wool socks, long underwear, lightweight wool sweater or acrylic sweatshirt, military surplus pants or jungle fatigues. But no, Mr. Know-It-All had chosen flannel shirts and Levi's and a leather jacket. He'd changed his soaked clothes for dry, but he was still chilled, fine tremors rippling through his body every few minutes.

It had taken them a few minutes to set up the tent after the skies opened up. Now the rain beat down on the plastic and sheeted off the sides, puddling on the ground outside. Inside the tent it smelled of rubber, damp wool, and something dank and moldering.

The money and backpack sat in the far corner. They had been through the backpack. No ID there either. No clue at all as to who the dead man was, but Taylor thought he fit the general description of Jon Jackson, one of the suspects in the Black Wolf Casino robbery. As a former employee of the casino, Jackson had come under investigation despite—or maybe partly because of—the fact that he'd left town two days before the robbery and hadn't been heard from since.

Will opened his mouth to tell—suggest—that Taylor change into his own spare fatigue pants, but Taylor said abruptly, "Only one hijacker got on that plane."

"Looks that way."

"One robber gets on the hijacked plane. The others split and go their separate ways."

"Maybe."

"Maybe. Either way, they go prop up their alibis—maybe they *are* each other's alibis."

Will scratched his bristling jaw, considering. Taylor was a natural at this kind of doublethink. In fact, he was a little too good. Some of his scenarios were straight out of Agatha Christie, in Will's opinion. But this one sounded reasonable: Wile E. Coyote leading the hounds off the trail of the foxes. Still, there were problems with it.

He said, "You think they trusted him to get on that plane and fly away with all that money? What happened to the 'no honor among thieves' rule?"

"I think it's more of a guideline. Anyway, it was a risk, sure. But it's not like they weren't the gambling kind."

Will acknowledged that.

Taylor said, "Getting that money out of town was one way of protecting it—and maybe protecting them—assuming they were local."

Will turned it over, nodded. "Maybe. Yeah, they couldn't take the risk of being stopped with the money, and they sure wouldn't want it turning up in any subsequent searches. They couldn't know how much time they'd have to stash it." He wished he could read Taylor's face, but Taylor was mostly staring out at the rain—and it was the first time Will had ever felt lonely in his company.

"They've probably spent every weekend up here since the snow started melting searching for that plane." He gave another of those little shivers.

Will said, "Maybe. Maybe they figure he double-crossed them."

Taylor finally glanced Will's way, his eyes oddly colorless—almost gray—in the dim light. "Maybe. But say they did some checking around. It probably wouldn't take long to figure out that no one ever saw Jackson after that night in December."

"If it was Jackson."

"They'd know the plane went down. I think they'd figure Jackson—yeah, if it was Jackson—and the money went down with it."

"It fits," Will agreed slowly.

He studied Taylor's sharply etched profile. It was hard to see in the fading light, but little details struck him: the black stubble on Taylor's jaw, the length of his eyelashes, the soft dark hair growing over his collar, the set line of his mouth. It was kind of a sexy mouth. Sensual, even a little pouty, though Taylor was not the pouty kind, and his mouth spent a lot more time laughing and shooting itself off at the wrong moment than it did pouting.

Taylor had his faults, God knew, but he was smart, savvy, and tough. He was good company most of the time; the best partner—the best friend—Will had ever had. He'd missed him badly these last six weeks. Hospital visits, even stopping by Taylor's place once he'd been released, hadn't been enough; in fact, it felt like he'd barely seen Taylor since the shooting.

The shooting.

It had been a routine op. Scratch that. It hadn't even officially been an op. They'd received a tip-off that a passport counterfeit ring was operating out of the back of a nail salon in Orange County's Little Saigon. A nail salon fronting a ring of counterfeiters? How dangerous could they be?

Will had been up front chatting pleasantly with the teenaged pink-haired receptionist, and sizing things up. Taylor was supposed to be out back scoping the alley and neighboring businesses—just getting the lay of the land. They had nothing to move on at that point; it was just intelligence gathering. But Taylor had wandered around to the back of the salon and slipped in through the delivery door, apparently deciding all on his own to take a look around. And whatever he'd spotted amidst the boxes of acrylic powders and foam rubber toe separators had encouraged him to poke around a little more in the stock room—which is where two juvenile members of the local Phu Fighters gang had found him.

The first clue Will had was the sound of shots from a back room in the salon. Two shots—and neither of them the familiar and distinct bang of Taylor's .357 SIG—and he'd known. Known instantly that Taylor had been shot.

He'd mown through the screaming, hysterical women, racing for the stockroom, and finding it—for one bewildered moment—empty. Then his gaze moved past the wall of boxes and metal shelving units and he'd spotted Taylor slumped on his side, blood spilling out of his chest, pooling on the cement floor. Taylor's face had been bone white with shock, his eyes huge and black and stunned. Will had knelt down beside him, kneeling in the puddle of Taylor's blood, and for one instant of sheer blind terror, he couldn't think beyond the fact that Taylor was dying. That any one of those shuddering, faint breaths might be his last.

It had never crossed his mind to go after the shooters. Not until later.

"Hang on, Taylor," he'd said, and he'd yelled at the terrified faces grouped in the doorway of the stockroom to call 911. His voice shook when he said, "Stay with me, Taylor. Stay." The words had seemed laden, charged with fears and feelings he'd never considered—never allowed himself to consider. And he'd shrugged out of his sports coat, putting it around Taylor, shouting at the women to bring him towels, clean towels to try to stanch the bleeding. And the frightened women had scattered, a couple of them returning with freshly laundered towels that he jammed up against the bullet wound in Taylor's chest.

Taylor's lashes had flickered. His colorless lips parted but no words came out, and Will didn't even know if Taylor could hear him or not. Taylor's eyes were open, pupils huge and black, but there was no other sign of consciousness in his chalky face, no response to Will. Will had taken Taylor's icy hand in his and chafed it, feeling the long, lax fingers twitch feebly; maybe it was response, maybe it was just…a dying nervous system shutting down for good. And it was the worst day, the worst hour, the worst moments of Will's life waiting for the paramedics—waiting for Taylor to stop breathing, for his eyes to fix and glaze before help could reach them.

But then, afterward, when it was clear that Taylor was going to live—and recover fully—Will had been…angry. Why not admit it? He had been angry. About as angry as he'd been terrified—which was about as terrified as he'd been in his life.

Because the truth was Taylor had brought it on himself. His ego hurt, he'd gone looking for trouble, and when he found it, he'd charged right into it without following procedure or using common sense. He hadn't waited for backup, and he sure as hell hadn't waited for Will. Taylor was a little headstrong and he was a little arrogant, but he wasn't stupid and he wasn't reckless—why had he done such a reckless, stupid, *stupid*, potentially fatally stupid thing?

And Will knew why. Because of David Bradley. Because Taylor found out Will was seeing David Bradley, and he'd been…jealous. Which didn't make a lick of sense. Taylor knew Will dated. Taylor dated. It was one of the first bonds between them: the fact that they were both gay. Not a lot of gay special agents in DSS. They'd have been a good team in any case, and they'd probably have been good friends—they shared a similar jaded worldview and sarcastic sense of humor—but the fact that they also shared the same sexual orientation… Yeah, it forged that bond between them into reinforced steel. They were practically brothers. Brothers-in-arms.

Less than two months ago Will would have said no one knew him better—no one was closer to him—than Taylor. That was assuming he'd have been willing to talk about his feelings—which he wouldn't have, of course. They didn't talk about that kind of thing.

Will glanced over at Taylor. Profile hard, he was staring out the tent window at the rain thundering down.

The last thing he'd ever meant to do was hurt Taylor.

He still wasn't clear exactly where he'd gone wrong.

He'd mentioned David in passing a few times, mentioned that he was seeing him. Taylor had seemed—well, he hadn't seemed anything in particular. Why would he? But that last afternoon, Will had mentioned he had seen David the night before, and Taylor had got kind of quiet and weird.

"You're seeing a lot of him," he'd said, bringing it up a couple of hours later when they stopped for lunch.

"Yeah? So?" Will had known immediately who Taylor meant; he knew Taylor too well to have missed that odd moment in the car earlier.

"You…getting serious?" And Taylor's face had been—well, frankly, Will still couldn't quite describe what Taylor's face had been. Troubled? Uncomfortable? Hurt? All of the above? It had been a weird expression, and it had been weirder yet because he could tell Taylor was trying not to show anything.

"Nah." But then he had made the fatal mistake of being honest. "I don't know."

And Taylor had gone white.

White.

Like Will had stabbed him. He looked stricken.

"What's the matter?" Will had said. "What's wrong?" Because something sure as hell was wrong.

But Taylor had laughed, closing up instantly—which wasn't how they were together. "Nothing's wrong. Bradley's a great guy." And he'd shrugged—like a guilty little kid caught in a lie. And then he'd changed the subject.

What. The. Hell.

But Will had let it drop—not like he had a choice. Taylor was talking himself away from the moment, whatever that moment had been. And, truth to tell, Will couldn't get away from that moment fast enough himself.

They'd been okay by the end of the day though, back in sync, back in step, and after their shift they'd gone for drinks at their favorite watering hole. Will should have realized then: Taylor was knocking back Rusty Nails like they were going out of style. His usual drink was beer. In fact, Taylor had a thing about trying every obscure import or microbrew out there. Whenever and wherever they traveled, Taylor had to try the local brew. The only time he ordered the hard stuff was when he was stressed—or people had done their best to maim or kill him.

But that night Taylor was putting the booze away like he had hollow legs. By the time Will had been ready to call it a day, Taylor was blasted: tie loosened, hair disheveled, giggling. *Giggling*, for chrissake. And, yeah, it was mildly cute: that boyish little gurgle, and those under-lashed looks Taylor was throwing him—like he was flirting with Will.

"Last call for you, buddy boy," Will had said, shaking his head, trying not to laugh when Taylor—leaning toward him—nearly fell off his stool.

And Taylor had draped an arm around Will's shoulders and drawled, "Take me to bed, William, or lose me forever!"

Will had laughed, although that kind of thing was risky as shit in what amounted to their local hangout. It was one thing to be gay; it was another to be openly gay. The last thing they needed was to buck for Federal GLOBE poster boys.

But Taylor was an affectionate drunk, no problems there, and he'd let Will steer him to Will's car, let Will drive him to Will's house, let Will walk him to the spare bedroom and help him undress—like they'd done for each other plenty of times in the past three years.

But then...then it had gotten hinky.

Taylor had put his arms around Will and said a lot of stupid things—drunken shit that Will had tried to ignore, tried to joke away—but Taylor had been insistent, if incoherent. They had wrestled around a little, Will losing patience maybe faster than he should have.

Because…he was tempted. He could admit that now. Sure, he'd been tempted—what with Taylor trying to nibble on his ear and all.

And it turned ugly fast—with the end result of Taylor grabbing his clothes and departing into the night.

The next day, for the first time in three years, they had nothing to say to each other. Maybe it would have worked itself out, but by lunchtime Taylor was in surgery with a bullet in his right lung, fighting for his life.

"It's letting up," he said, jolting Will out of his thoughts. "The rain," Taylor said, meeting Will's blank gaze.

"We could make camp here tonight," Will heard himself say. It made sense. He and Taylor had to get things straight between them, and that wasn't going to happen once they got back to civilization.

But Taylor was already crawling out of the tent. "May as well keep moving," he said. "We've got a lot of ground to cover."

* * * * *

The light was amazing. Those crepuscular rays—golden shafts of illumination—penetrating the snowy rafters of clouds. What did they call those? Jacob's ladder? The fields around them were bathed in amber, the trees glinting and flashing in the dueling sun and shade. The surrounding mountains looked purple and blue.

With cold, probably.

Taylor put that thought away. As long as he kept moving he was warm enough, and it looked like they would be moving till nightfall. But that had been his choice. All he had to do was say the word and Will would be fussing over him like a hen with one chick. And the sad thing was, there was a part of him that would have almost enjoyed that.

He glanced at Will walking a little ahead. His face was flushed with sun and exertion, his eyes sparkled—despite everything, he was enjoying himself. Will was totally in his element out here. He liked the silence, the emptiness, the loneliness. He'd have been perfectly happy on his own, whereas nothing but Will would have dragged Taylor out to this wilderness—beautiful as it was.

He shivered as a gust of wind—tasting of snow and distant mountaintops—hit him. Will glanced his way, but said nothing.

* * * * *

"I think we should stash the money," Taylor said, breaking the silence of nearly an hour. He was trailing two or three yards behind Will, and Will was glad to have a reason to stop and take a look at him. He looked beat, and it pissed Will off, made his voice sharper than it needed to be.

"What are you talking about?"

"I don't know if waltzing into a sheriff's station with two million dollars is a good idea."

Will stared, trying to see it from whatever angle Taylor was viewing this. "You think someone in the sheriff's department was involved?"

"I don't know." Even Taylor's voice was tired. "I just know it's a small town, a lot of money, and the sheriffs didn't seem to make a lot of headway on the case."

"Well, hell, neither did the FBI."

Taylor didn't say anything. Will's dad had been a small town sheriff in Oregon, and Will knew what Taylor thought: that Will was on defense because of that—and maybe Taylor was right.

"Okay. What's your idea?" he asked grudgingly.

"We could leave the money in one of these bear boxes, contact the feds —"

Will spluttered, "Leave two million dollars in a *bear box*?"

"Just hear me out."

Blue eyes met green.

"We could put the money in my pack. I don't have a dry change of clothes left and you're carrying half my gear anyway —"

Will had opened his mouth but he shut it at that.

"Whatever else I need—my pistol—I can carry."

"And what if someone steals your backpack?"

"The kind of people who hike back into these mountains aren't even the same species as the sewer rats we deal with. Besides, we've seen…what? Two hikers and one park ranger since we set out? I don't think anyone's going to rip off my pack. But…I'll leave my ID."

"What?"

Taylor sighed. "Just listen a minute. It's only for about forty-eight hours, and we're basically alone on this mountain. But say some lowlife does go through my gear. My ID acts as a kind of hands-off. You've gotta be pretty hard-core to tangle with the federal government—which is what my ID amounts to."

"That is the dumbest damn idea I've ever heard." But even as Will was saying it, he was thinking that Taylor did have a point. Leaving his ID in his backpack was about as clear a staking of claim, a warning, as there was—and he was also right about the unlikelihood of their running into anyone. Even so…

He said, "And then the feds have to hike up here to retrieve the cash?"

"Come off it, Brandt. They have to anyway. There's the crash site, the body—this hill is going to be crawling with law enforcement in seventy-two hours. There won't be any possibility of the money slipping through the cracks."

"That would have to be a pretty big crack for two million dollars to slip through."

"Yeah, well, sorry if I don't feel like taking a chance when it's your name and mine attached."

"You are one paranoid sonofabitch." But Will was grinning, amused, and in a weird way, pleased by these nutty Machiavellian maneuverings. It was so…Taylor.

And Taylor gave him a little sideways grin, acknowledging the compliment like a pretty girl accepting roses.

* * * * *

The bear box was a long and low metal trunk painted a particularly ugly shade of brown. The campground was deserted, and Taylor's pack was on its own as he stowed it, and locked the lid.

Will was shaking his head, but he had decided it didn't hurt taking this extra precaution—and, frankly, they could move faster if Taylor didn't have to lug a fifty-five pound backpack.

"Did you want to camp here tonight?" he asked. The shadows were lengthening, the air growing chillier. They were going to have to call it a day shortly anyway.

"Let's keep moving." Taylor was already heading for the trail.

And Will couldn't help the edge that crept into his voice. "I didn't realize you were in such a big hurry to get back."

Taylor just gave him one of those long looks, aloof and wronged at the same time. It aggravated Will—but then Taylor seemed to do that without any effort these days. It didn't make sense. He and Taylor had always got along well; even in the ways that they were unalike they used to complement each other. It was just since the shooting that everything was different. Will didn't *want* it to be different. He wanted things to go back to the way they had been.

His eyes rested a moment on Taylor's wide shoulders, moved down to his narrow hips and long legs.

Damn Taylor for ever opening this Pandora's box because while it was true Will had refused to ever consider sleeping with his partner and friend—the best partner and the best friend he'd ever had—it wasn't like he had failed to notice how…hot…Taylor was. He'd have to have been blind to have missed it. Taylor was sexy as sin. Sexy, funny, smart, capable—all the things Will wanted in a lover. But besides being Will's partner and best friend, he was commitment-shy and had the mating instincts of a young gazelle. He was a bad relationship risk for anyone, but in particular he was a bad risk for Will.

Will liked stability, reliability, predictability. He needed those things.

All the same, turning Taylor down that night at his house had been one of the hardest things Will had ever done—and if Taylor hadn't been definitely the worse for alcohol, Will wasn't totally confident he'd have managed it.

He'd put the thought out of his mind during the long weeks of Taylor's recuperation, but now that Taylor was looking and acting more like his old self—and continuing to put himself on offer—Will was starting to have trouble.

Like...in his dreams at night.

The visuals were bad enough, but in his dreams it was the smell, the taste, the *feel* of callused hands sliding over ridged abdominals, cut pectorals, taut nipples—smooth skin and soft hair—the damp tangle of groin, fingers wrapping around a hot, rigid shaft. In the dream he was initiating and experiencing at the same time, as if there were no division, no separation between where he ended and Taylor began.

That wasn't a dream; that was a nightmare.

And a bigger nightmare was the fact that even in broad daylight it was a struggle keeping his mind off the thought of having Taylor—or, for that matter, Taylor having him. And how weird was that? Will didn't enjoy bottoming for anyone, but the idea of *Taylor*...imagining the exquisite shock of that full body contact, of strength equal to his pleasuring him, owning him. It made him half-hard just thinking about it, his face heating up in a way that made him grateful that Taylor had turned away again.

* * * * *

The terrain had changed quite a bit from that morning: sun-baked bluffs and stony slopes giving way to chinquapin shrubs and manzanita which yielded in turn to hillsides of oaks and conifers leading to a series of meadows and lakes.

After leaving the junction campsite, they followed a trail which descended the north wall of East Hancock Gorge. The drop was moderate at first but ended with a series of steep, rocky switchbacks.

Taylor's legs were shaking by the time they reached the bottom of a long trench where a green and sparkling tributary tumbled in a suicidal fall off the mountainside. They still had that mountainside to get down, and he was glad he wasn't carrying his pack—in fact, it seemed worth two million dollars to have unloaded it. He was cold, he was hungry, and he was depressed.

Even the thought of having recovered the money from the Black Wolf Casino heist didn't particularly cheer him up; maybe Will had a point if recovering a couple of million dollars felt less important than the rift in their partnership. Maybe his priorities were getting screwed up. At this point he was too tired to care.

He followed Will down a narrow, deeply shaded trail to a clearing where white steam rose in the rain-swept air from what looked like a rough, rock-ringed pool. Will stopped and lowered his pack, so apparently they were taking another break, and thank Jesus for that. At this point, a few weeks of being stuck on desk duty sounded like paradise.

"Junction Hot Springs," Will said. "There used to be a hotel a few miles down the mountain. I think it's a private lodge now. If it's still there at all."

"A hotel *here?*"

"It was a health resort. People used to come up here for the fresh air and massage and the miracle waters."

Taylor was rolling his head from side to side on his shoulders, trying to work out a crick. "I wouldn't mind a massage." He heard the echo of his voice, and just managed to avoid looking at Will.

After a minute, Will said, "Well, how about a hot bath anyway? Get you nice and warmed up, take the ache out of your muscles."

Will was already pulling his olive drab sweater over his head, followed by his thermal top, and then his snowy white T-shirt. Beneath all the layers, his chest was brown and smooth, the soft dark hair bisecting his taut, muscular torso and disappearing beneath the band of his camo pants.

"Are you serious?"

"Yeah. We could both use it." Unself-consciously—and why should he be self-conscious? They'd dressed and undressed in front of each other plenty of times—Will stepped out of his pants and boxers, lowering cautiously to the man-made cement bench inside the pool.

Hands propped on his hips, Taylor studied him, but Will just sighed and closed his eyes, putting his head back. "Come on, MacAllister," he murmured. "Relax for five minutes."

Swearing under his breath, Taylor peeled off his vest, flannel shirt, T-shirt and wriggled out of his Levi's. Will ignored him, still soaking, face skyward while the steam drifted up around him.

Taylor slid into the water and yelped, standing up and preparing to jump right back out. "Jesus, it's boiling!"

Will's eyes opened. "It's about one hundred and fifteen degrees." Will was a stickler for accuracy. He always insisted on looking over Taylor's reports before he handed them in—not that Taylor was any less accurate—but Will was a little bit of a control freak. "Stay still," he advised. He was flushed and perspiring, but on him it looked good. Sexy. But then Will looked sexy whether he was staring down the barrel of an M4 or eating a sloppy joe.

Taylor leveled him a look but held motionless, giving his body time to adjust to the heat. Finally, he eased the rest of the way down on the stone bench and sank back, the water level rising as he did, sloshing gently back against Will, who stretched his arms out along the back of the tub.

The steam settled on Taylor's face, and his forehead broke out in sweat. He breathed in deeply, hot moisture invading his nostrils.

Will smiled lazily.

Taylor spread his legs, the water rippling gently with his motion, and let the wet heat suffuse every part of his body. Yeah, that was better. The water was silky soft, and now the heat felt caressing, sinking into every pore, every cavity. Startling, but good. In fact, it was the first time he'd felt really warm in days.

He glanced over and Will was staring. He looked down. His chest was still a mess of scars beneath the soft dusting of returning hair. The scars would fade in time but they were ugly now. He let himself slip lower into the water, hiding the ugliness from Will.

Will's eyes moved to his face, and Taylor said, "This was a good idea."

Will nodded.

"Finally," Taylor added, and Will chuckled and kicked water his way. And because Taylor was lying so low, he took a wave of hot mineral water in the face—which couldn't go without retaliation.

A second later Will was the one with his hair plastered down his face. He whipped his hair back and laughed. Water sparkled on the tips of his eyelashes and his teeth were very white.

"You're living dangerously, buddy boy."

Taylor lazily flipped his foot, spattering Will with smoky wet.

"Bring it on, cowboy," he drawled.

Will dived for him and they grappled amiably, hands slipping on slick bodies, tussling and twisting in the steaming water. They stepped on each other's feet, but avoided kneeing anything vital, the rough stone scraping their backs and butts—panting and laughing.

Finally, Taylor managed to wriggle free, and half-lunged, half-waded over to the other side of the tub. Will turned his head to spit out the water he'd swallowed. "Hey," he said. "Do you have any protection?"

Taylor bit back a grin, scissoring his legs through the water. "You think I'll need more than the SIG to keep you back?"

"Funny," Will said. "I mean, do you have a condom with you?"

He was serious. Taylor stilled. All at once his heart was pounding very fast. He managed to keep his tone lazy as he asked, "Is this a trick question?"

Will said slowly, "Well, we could get it out of our system."

It took Taylor a moment to absorb that one.

Finally he managed, "Gee, and they say romance is dead."

"You want to, right? That's what you said. That's what it was all about, right?"

Taylor's eyes narrowed. "It wasn't just about fucking."

"No?" Will's smile was cynical.

"No."

Will moved next to Taylor on the rock bench, put a wet hand on Taylor's shoulder, tugging him over. A warm, possessive handprint breaking apart in tiny drops, rolling down Taylor's skin; it had no power over him—yet he let himself be drawn into Will's arms.

CHAPTER FOUR

"I don't know about this," Taylor said gruffly.

Which was kind of funny considering how hard he'd pushed for it on one notable occasion.

And even funnier considering how his body was already reacting to the proximity of Will's.

Will's muscular arms felt good about him; the last time he had held Taylor this tight they had been fighting for real, and Taylor had wanted to kill him. But now Will's arms felt friendly, familiar, and although he was asking for something Taylor wasn't sure he could give, he felt no need to fight, to force his release.

Will asked, "You want it, don't you?"

The words came out a little aggressively, and Taylor considered him for a moment. "Yeah."

"Well?"

"Well, what? This is kind of a sudden change of heart, isn't it?"

"I never said I didn't find you attractive. In fact, I said I *did* find you attractive. I just didn't think it was a good idea for us."

"Because we partners. And because we're friends."

"That's right." Will's gaze was cool and a little hard. "But you disagree. And who am I to argue? Maybe you're right."

Taylor's brows drew together.

"I'll tell you one thing," Will said. "Ever since that night I haven't been able to get the idea out of my head. I want you." His big hand slid over Taylor's flat belly, fingertips reaching. Taylor's cock was already stiff and swollen, anticipating that touch. "And you sure as hell want me."

Yeah, there was no hiding that fact. Taylor bit his lip as Will's hand fastened around his cock, trying to withhold the revealing groan threatening to tear out of his chest. Just...*that* felt so good. Just Will's hand on him. But he forced himself to try to think.

"And what happens afterward? Are you going to regret it? Maybe blame me?"

As though in answer, Will's hand pumped him—just once—down and up, fist brushing Taylor's belly and then sliding up to the sensitive glans. Taylor shuddered all over. *"Will..."*

Will's hands were moving over him, and instinctively Taylor cooperated, rising and letting himself be positioned between Will's powerful thighs. He could feel Will's half-erect cock nudging his backside as Will's arms around his waist drew him back. And the sad thing was it felt...good having this taken out of his hands. What did that say about him? But he'd been wanting it—yearning for it—for *so* long...

"Listen," Will said, his breath warm and steamy against Taylor's ear, "we already know each other, care about each other. This isn't going to change that, but I think it might settle something once and for all. For both of us."

Taylor was silent. He could feel Will watching him, waiting.

"You really think I'm just curious about what it would be like with you?" he asked finally.

"I think you want me. I think we've established I want you too," Will said. "But, sure, I think there's an element of curiosity in it, and I think if we take care of that...we'll be able to get back to business."

Taylor chuckled, although there wasn't a lot of humor in it. "Either you don't have a lot of faith in yourself or you're seriously underestimating my charms." He put his hands over Will's wrists, feeling the muscles move in Will's forearms.

Will said soberly, as though he were paying Taylor a compliment, "I know the partnership, the friendship means more to you than…this."

"That's easy to say when we haven't done *this* yet."

Will chuckled, his breath tickling the back of Taylor's neck. "But we're going to," he said. Beneath Taylor's hands, Will's arms were hard, muscular bands around Taylor's waist, holding him close, but Taylor knew if he wanted free he could have it in a minute. Will was crowding him, yeah, but he wasn't going to force him. Taylor could still say no. And if he had any sense at all, that's what he'd do because Will really had no clue what he was talking about.

But Taylor didn't push away. Instead he leaned back into Will's arms, resting his head against Will's broad shoulder and tipping his face up at the sullen sky. He could feel Will's surprise, feel his grip change instantly to support, automatically offering Taylor harbor. And it was surprisingly relaxing to…acquiesce just this much. To yield to the combined pressure of Will's desire and his own. Will's arms cradled him, his strength reassuring rather than challenging, while Taylor tried to decide whether he wanted to take this to the next level.

Oh, there was no question that he wanted to. But he didn't want to take this at the expense of further damaging his relationship with Will. And that could so easily happen, regardless of what Will said now—because Will wasn't looking at this realistically. Which was kind of funny, considering the fact that Will believed himself to be the practical, hardheaded one. But right now he was letting his other head rule.

"I didn't bring a condom," Taylor lied at last, reluctantly—and started to sit up.

Will's voice was unexpectedly harsh. "I did."

Taylor jerked around, water swirling, and Will let him go.

"Is that so?" He couldn't help the edge that came into his voice. "You always carry one?"

Will shrugged. "I noticed it in my pack last night."

Taylor absorbed this, trying to remember the last time Will had gone camping and who he'd gone with; he decided he'd be happier not thinking about it.

"Always prepared, huh?"

"Something like that." Will's gaze challenged him in some indefinable way.

The idea of Will with someone else settled it for Taylor. Sexual jealousy was the wrong reason to fuck your best friend and closest colleague, but —

He turned his back, pushing against the prod of Will's erection, instinctively encouraging that stiffening swell, forgetting all about the fact that this was probably a bad idea. Pushing away the thought that this wasn't even like Will really—and that Will was probably going to regret it—and that was going to hurt worse than not doing it at all. Will's cock scraped lightly down the crack of Taylor's ass, probing or maybe just moving with the water.

"Is that what you want?" Will's breath was cool compared to the steam.

He wanted—well, there wasn't one single thing he wanted. He'd have liked to bury himself up to his balls in Will's taut tanned ass, but Will returning the favor would be as good in a different way—maybe even better because Will might like it more like that, might remember it—and want to do it again sometime. Besides, just for one hour, he'd like to feel like he belonged to Will. He already knew Will didn't belong to him, but to belong to Will—would be good. Even if just for a little while.

"Yeah," he said huskily. "That's what I want."

"I want it too," Will grated. "I want to fuck you. Hard."

Taylor dipped his head, swallowed. He'd always pictured Will as a gentle lover, playful—teasing. There was a hint of anger in Will's tone that he didn't get, but he nodded his agreement anyway. The idea of Will taking him hard was weirdly exciting.

"Yeah, fuck me," he whispered. "Hard."

He jerked in surprise as Will bit his shoulder. It hurt. But then Will kissed the bite mark so sweetly. He shivered. He didn't want Will kissing him—that was liable to break his heart.

The smart thing would be to pull away, get himself on the other side of this tub, and laugh it off. But Will's arm was locked around him again—he wasn't going anywhere easily. Instead he lifted his hips as Will's free hand arrowed down the hard curve of Taylor's butt cheek, a friendly sweep of caress that ended with one finger poked right up into Taylor's pursed little hole.

Surprise.

He couldn't help his body's instinctive arch and the little guttural moan of stung pleasure.

"Jesus, Will…you could've…" But he was suddenly out of oxygen. The stroking motion of Will's finger made a funny suction with the water, and set the sphincter muscle fluttering in time to the butterfly beat of Taylor's heart. *"Oh…"* He closed his eyes. That wash of hot water and knowing press on spongy tissue. Will had big hands. Hard hands. Thick fingers and callused palms, and he was probing Taylor deeply, his touch possessive, knowing.

Too knowing. And abruptly Taylor wanted to fight that exquisite invasion. He didn't let anyone do this to him. Not ever. He was always the one in charge, the one who called the shots. He was the predator, not the prey. What the hell was he doing giving in to this?

He tried to pull back a little, but Will held him in place and thrust his finger in and out of Taylor's hole, delicately and ruthlessly finger fucking him. Taylor groaned, trying to angle his body, telling himself he was pulling away, but helplessly pushing back on Will's hand.

What was happening to him? Will was making him feel too much, too intensely. He was giving up control—no, admit it, control was being taken from him. That finger shoving even deeper in his body, forcing him to feel and respond. He bit his lip, trying not to cry out, to beg for more.

Will was going to make him come—just like that, and despite the dizzy pleasure, Taylor began to get mad. This wasn't what he'd wanted. He hadn't surrendered his will for this impersonal manipulation. He wanted Will's cock inside his body, not his hand. He wanted Will feeling it too, helpless with it, not playing him. He grabbed his dick and began to work himself, needing to control his body's reaction, to at least control his own orgasm.

"Next time I'm doing *you*," he warned roughly. He focused on his own hands, what he was doing to himself, fighting to bring himself back under control.

Will's other arm let him go; he felt Will twisting, groping outside the pool, and then the tear of foil but it was distant because he just couldn't seem to think beyond that finger—two fingers now—pushing knowledgably inside his body, stroking and massaging him. Well, he'd said he wanted a massage, hadn't he? Not quite what he'd pictured. His hands rested weak and heavy on his groin.

"I don't want —" His breath caught raggedly, and against his best intentions he was shoving back, craving that touch buried in his body.

"Yeah, you do. You're desperate for it. You don't fool me," Will murmured. "If you were a cat you'd be purring." He wriggled his fingers, and Taylor, still trying to preserve the illusion of self-command, snarled. Will chuckled, but the joke was on Taylor because Will deliberately changed his angle and the pressure, and Taylor's voice cut off on a sound that was embarrassingly kittenish.

To distract himself he began to pump his cock again, water splashing, forcing himself to action.

"No you don't. Not without me you don't." Will heaved up, giving him a little bounce to break his concentration. "Wait for me."

Taylor groaned in frustration as Will moved around some more, and then suddenly Will half picked him up, one powerful arm clamped around Taylor's waist, shifting Taylor's slick, buoyant body. A few errant pokes at balls and cheeks, and without more warning than that, Will's cock pushed inside.

Taylor froze at the shock of it. Never. Never before had he let this happen. He had another guy's cock crammed in his ass. He was letting another guy take him. He shook with the pain and confusion of it.

Will was groaning. "Christ God almighty, Taylor..." His voice sounded desperate. On the edge of tears. Will was more shocked than Taylor was—and Taylor calmed a little, listening, absorbing the truth of that.

Will trembled with the effort of holding motionless, but Taylor could feel his heart thundering behind his own, and any fear that he was alone in this, that he had relinquished too much for too little, faded. He winced—wriggled, trying to accommodate that thick rigidity. Water was not enough of a lubricant. What had they been thinking?

"Are you okay?" Will sounded hoarse. He rocked against Taylor—stopped himself—then rocked again like he just couldn't help it. "Say...something."

To his astonishment, Taylor heard himself whimper. A helpless little submissive sound—and he nudged his ass against Will's groin in clear invitation.

WTF? *Literally* WTF.

And Will responded instantly, unleashed, thrusting in fierce, deep strokes into Taylor's tight channel, grunting softly like it was a fight, like he was taking body blows.

And Taylor responded by humping back, making those helpless little encouraging cries. Pushing, shoving, insisting.

Well, he'd asked for it, and now he was getting it, impaled on Will's cock and getting fucked hard and thoroughly. And there wasn't a damn thing he could do about it, mostly because he didn't want to do a damn thing about it. Will slammed into him, setting the pace—hard and fast—and Taylor raced to catch up, begging for more, just about wild with it. But at least it was mutual now. Both of them out of control with pleasure and pain and longing and bewilderment. This was *them.* And everything Taylor believed he knew about their partnership was taking a beating.

Splish, splash, he was pounding my ass…

He giggled a little hysterically and Will laughed too, a breathless huff. "You…crazy…bastard…"

And now Taylor had the rhythm, sliding up and down the length of Will's cock while he grabbed himself hard and jerked off under water, making a little turbulence like the struggles of a ship going down or a drowning sailor sinking under for the last time.

Their sweat hit the water in glistening droplets, steam rising. It was moist and hot and sexy as all get out although they were probably alarming the hell out of the local wildlife.

Taylor was bumping and grinding, trying not to lose the pace, wrestling Will for control. And Will fighting every step of the way, insisting on command. It was frenetic. Sensation started at the base of his cock and spine and sparkled up through nerves and muscle.

Will cursed under his breath and bit the vulnerable join of Taylor's neck and shoulder. Taylor choked back another gasp of something between a laugh and a sob, and then Will's hand covered his, pumping him frantically.

He was a little surprised when Will's face nudged his, Will's mouth latching on, sweet and hot and hungry. Oh, God. Kisses from Will. His chest tightened in crazy emotional response.

He'd known it would be sweet, but this was almost unbearable, his heart swelling with so much…*feeling* for Will. Such a terrible tenderness and longing and…love.

And then Will cried out, something broken and inarticulate that Taylor swallowed. He could feel the throb of Will's orgasm thrumming through his own body, hot water and rubber pushing into him and spilling right out again, and he was sorry it wasn't just their bodies, silk-skinned steel, but it was still so good —

Flagging, Will thrust against him again, sharply, once... twice...

He began to come himself, spurting into the water, a milky cloud that evaporated as if it had never been.

It was over so quickly. Not fair at all considering how long he'd waited for it.

But his own erection was wilting fast, shriveling down to nothing in the water, and after a few moments he felt Will's rigid length soften and then slip out of his body.

Will was turning him, pulling him into his arms, holding him tightly, burying his flushed, perspiring face in Taylor's throat.

"Yeah, you're right," Taylor said shakily, locking his arms around Will's shoulders, hugging him back tightly. "No big deal."

"Christ, shut up," Will said unsteadily.

"Thank God we did this. Now we don't have to ever think about it again."

"If you don't want me to drown you, shut up," Will said. He was laughing, but his laugh cracked.

* * * * *

It was twilight when they reached the bottom of the trail descending to the next canyon.

"We'll make camp here tonight," Will said as though expecting an argument, but Taylor just nodded. What was there to argue about? He was worn out, and Will's silence since they had left Junction Hot Springs unnerved him.

He'd known it would be a mistake to give in to that sexual hunger, but he'd sort of hoped it would take Will longer than three minutes to regret it. Apparently not.

They set up the tent in silence, and Will got the campfire going while Taylor collected loose firewood. The smell of wood smoke and coffee was sweet in the evening air and the stars were already faintly glimmering in the indigo and pink sky. He brought an armload of wood back, dumping it with relief.

"Coffee ready?"

"Not yet." Will handed Taylor his flask. "Here. Have a slug of this." He was watching Taylor in a way that made him self-conscious. Taylor raised his brows and Will turned away abruptly.

Great.

Taylor handed back the flask, but Will had already moved away—the line of his back unencouraging. Taylor put the flask in the breast pocket of his shirt.

It took effort not to say *I told you so.* Maybe that was funny coming from him because he had been the one originally pushing for this—except he had never been pushing for sex as a goal in itself. That was the thing Will had never understood about him.

"What'd you want tonight?" Will asked a short time later, rifling through the contents of his pack.

Taylor opened his mouth, then caught Will's expression and decided a joke would be a mistake. Will was just waiting for him to say something—the wrong thing.

"Whatever you want. I'm not particular." He was serious—and he was talking about their freeze-dried menu—but Will's face tightened.

"Right. We need to talk," he said grimly.

Words every man dreaded hearing—even when they came from another man.

Taylor said desperately, "How much can there be to say about dehydrated turkey tetrazzini, Brandt?"

"That's not what I mean."

Shit. There was no kidding around when Will got in this mood. He gave up fighting the inevitable, folded his arms on his knees, waiting.

"Shoot." He couldn't help adding, "But not literally, okay?"

That was just nerves talking, but there wasn't a glimmer of a smile from Will. "We can't go on like this, MacAllister."

A little irritably—wasn't this what he'd been saying all along?—he said, "Yeah, I know."

"Okay, maybe sex wasn't the point. Maybe you were right about that much."

"Well, no kidding."

"Do you really want to break up the team?"

Taylor exhaled a long breath, staring at his hands. He said finally, reluctantly, "I think it would be for the best."

Was that really what he thought? Because saying it felt like the end of the world. And the silence that followed didn't make it any easier.

Finally, Will said, "Is that really what you think or is this some kind of—I don't know. An ultimatum?"

Taylor searched inside himself. Tried to put aside his own feelings and figure out what he expected of Will. He was forced to conclude that he did not expect anything. He had always understood that Will did not want to get involved—not with his partner—not at the expense of their team. If they had met under other circumstances...well, probably not then, either, because Will was convinced that Taylor was incapable of a relationship that lasted longer than fifteen minutes. Will just did not believe that Taylor was his type, and who would know better? So Taylor knew what he wanted was unrealistic. It was really out of curiosity that he asked, "If it was an ultimatum, what would your answer be?"

Will groaned, put his head in his hands. "What kind of fucking question is that?" Lowering his hands, he sighed. It was a long, weary sound. "I don't know. Maybe you *are* right. I was hoping this afternoon might settle some things..."

"Did it settle something for you?" Taylor asked, and he couldn't help the note that crept into his voice because he thought if Will said yes he was totally bullshitting himself. It had been crazy, but it had also been fantastic between them, and Taylor was certainly experienced enough to know the feelings hadn't been all on his side.

But Will didn't answer that. He just said, "If you still feel like…you want out…"

He opened his mouth to deny that it was what he wanted, but that was what it amounted to. As painful as the idea of breaking the partnership was, he couldn't go on working side by side with Will feeling the way he did. The idea of watching the David Bradleys come and go in Will's life, or worse, watching Will settle down with someone like David Bradley—who, in fairness, was a perfectly decent guy—was more than he could take.

It wasn't reasonable or logical on his part, but…

Maybe he *was* as self-centered and egotistical as Will thought. As embarrassing as that was to admit.

And maybe fucking in a hot tub had settled everything nicely for Will, but it had just confirmed for Taylor what he already knew. He wasn't getting over this anytime soon.

He said carefully, "This way we walk away friends. Which matters to me. A lot. The way we were going… I don't know that we would."

The truth of that was in Will's eyes. After a very long moment, he nodded.

Which settled that.

They moved about the camp getting ready for the night, and every time Taylor looked at Will's closed expression his chest ached in a way that had nothing to do with cold air in his healing lung.

"Did you really want the turkey tetrazzini?" Will asked politely when the water had boiled.

"I was just kidding," Taylor returned, equally polite.

They ate beef stew in silence. They had cleared the air, but there didn't seem to be much to say any more. Taylor couldn't even work up enough enthusiasm to discuss their dead hijacker and casino heist.

The stars came out: incredibly huge and bright in the black skies. It got colder. They were both tired, and Taylor knew he wasn't alone in not wanting to squeeze into that little tent and lie there listening to each other pretend to sleep.

"Anything else you want out of my pack?" Will asked finally. "Toothpaste? Soap? Anything else to eat?"

"No, I'm fine."

"I guess I'll bear bag everything."

Taylor nodded, but Will made no move to get up and hang the food and items that might attract bears. He poked the campfire with a stick, his grim face half in shadow, half in rosy light. He could have been a million miles away, sitting on that distant pockmarked moon rising over the serrated tips of the mountains.

Taylor shivered—and for once Will didn't notice. Taylor rose. Will didn't look up. He opened his mouth, but he didn't know what to say. Instead, he went to get his jacket out of the tent. It was colder tonight, and the air was damp. The night air, spicy with pines and wood smoke, smelled like more rain was on the way. Looking at their sleeping bags lying there side by side gave him a funny feeling in the pit of his stomach.

His SIG was lying on his bag, and he remembered his joke about using it to keep Will back.

Shrugging on his jacket, Taylor crawled back out of the tent.

Will was watching him. He said suddenly, "Look, Taylor. What if we…tried to…I don't know. Take it one day at a time?"

He looked like a stranger, bearded, his eyes shining with a mystery emotion. He looked intense, urgent.

Bushes to the side of Taylor rustled, and something twittering flew up and winged away into the night. When he looked back, Will was on his feet—waiting for his answer, apparently. He wasn't even sure what the question was.

As he stared, Will shrugged. Said offhandedly, "We could try, right? It would be worth trying."

Taylor opened his mouth to ask what they were going to try, exactly, but there was motion to his left and—and then to the right—and a couple of shadows detached themselves from the darkness and walked into the ring of campfire light.

CHAPTER FIVE

There were three of them. Two men and a woman—although it took Taylor a moment to identify her as such beneath the shapeless clothing. They wore hunting caps, heavy plaid jackets, and they carried rifles. Taylor didn't know much about it, but he was pretty sure hunting was not allowed in a national park.

He barely caught himself from reaching for his missing shoulder holster, instead throwing Will a look, and what he read in Will's face confirmed that they were in trouble—even before the trio moved across the open space of the campsite, cutting him off from his partner.

"Evening," said one of the men. He was older than his companions, sixty or so, but he looked trim and fit—and very alert. "We saw your campfire."

The second man was tall, six-three, maybe six-four. Big. He had long blond curls beneath the duck-billed hunting cap. He stepped toward Taylor, staring at his boots.

"It's him. I'm bettin' it's him."

"You mind?" the older man said to Taylor.

"Do I mind what?" Taylor asked warily.

"The sole of your boot. Let's see it."

Taylor thought of the .357 SIG lying on his sleeping bag in the tent. Three short steps away.

But they'd still be outgunned. Will's 9mm was probably in his backpack, and although these were close quarters for rifles, all three were handling their weapons with the ease of long practice. Taylor counted two suppressed .22 rifles and one semiautomatic with a scope.

He lifted his leg, offering them a gander at the mountain grip outsole of his Adidas Badpak GTX, balancing for a moment in a way that felt way too *Karate Kid* for comfort.

"It's him!" the younger man exclaimed. "That's the boot that made the tracks around the plane."

"Nice job, Cinderella," Will said calmly, and Taylor understood that Will was letting him know that he understood the situation as Taylor did, that he was ready and waiting for opportunity to present itself.

"Hands on the back of your head, son," instructed the older man—clearly the leader—to Taylor. Taylor clasped his hands behind his head. "Search him, Stitch."

The woman kept her rifle trained on Will while the younger man yanked Taylor around, searching him roughly.

"We've been tracking you two most of the day," the older man said, watching this procedure closely. "You were making pretty good time until you decided to go skinny-dipping."

The woman laughed.

At that moment Taylor was glad he couldn't see Will's face.

"It's not on him," Stitch said, and he emphasized his disappointment by shoving Taylor down.

Taylor rolled with it, coming up on his knee. Ready, but too far away to do anything—especially with a rifle trained on Will.

"Well, well," the older man said, observing this. "What circus did you escape from?"

"Where's the money?" Stitch yelled, and he kicked at Taylor, who grabbed his foot and twisted, throwing the other man flat. He didn't have opportunity to follow up, though, because the other two rifles cocked simultaneously—one pointed at him and one pointed at Will's head.

"Stitch, would you stop fooling around," the older man said wearily. "Is he carrying any ID?"

"Nothin'," Stitch said, climbing to his feet. "Not a damn thing." He reached down, fastening his massive hands in Taylor's coat, dragging him up and punching him in the belly.

Taylor doubled over, beef stew and bile rising in his throat. He managed to stay on his feet, although that was partly because Stitch still had hold of his jacket.

Through the pain he heard the older man saying, "Here's the problem. We believe you two have something that belongs to us."

"I don't know what the hell it would be," Will said, his voice tight with anger.

"Put your hands behind your head! That plane that you walked round and around and climbed into and walked around some more yesterday? That plane was carrying something that belonged to us, and we want it back."

"If you mean the pilot, he's right where you left him," Taylor got out, muffled. His head was down so he didn't see the punch that caught him under the ribs. He cried out, the pain catching him by surprise; it hurt much worse than the slug to the gut, thanks to his damaged ribs. He remembered the doctor's warning about his healing lung being vulnerable to detaching from his rib cage again, and he thought he'd shut up for a bit. He coughed a couple of times and tried not to throw up.

"Look," Will said, "whatever you think —"

"Son, you move another muscle and I'll blow your goddamned head off," the older man interrupted. "Search him."

The woman went quickly, clumsily through the layers of Will's clothes. She pulled out a baggie—Will's ID carefully water and weatherproofed—dangled it in the firelight, and then nearly dropped it.

"Orrin," she called.

The older man backed up, still keeping his rifle trained on Will. Taylor was grateful for that unobstructed view of Will. Will was watching Orrin and the woman, but his eyes slid sideways, meeting Taylor's, and just that went a long way to calming Taylor.

The woman was hissing—like Will and Taylor shouldn't hear this?—"He's a *cop.* A *fed.* Special Agent Will Brandt. He's with the Bureau of Diplomatic Security."

"What the hell is Diplomatic Security?" Stitch asked. "They supposed to be diplomats or something?"

"Yeah, we're diplomats," Taylor muttered, forgetting his resolve to keep his mouth shut.

"Oh yeah, where's your embassy?"

"Oh, for chrissake," the woman said. *"Orrin."*

Orrin said to Taylor, "You're a fed too, I guess."

Taylor said nothing.

"That's quite a coincidence. Two federal agents just happen to be up here camping off-season?"

"We're on vacation," Will said. "It's a national park. A lot of people are camping here."

"Not here, they're not."

Unfortunately, he was right about that.

"Search the tent, Stitch." Orrin trained his rifle on Taylor, who was still leaning over, hands braced on his thighs, practicing breathing.

Feeling Will's gaze, Taylor looked up again, tried to reassure him with his eyes that he was okay, and ready to back Will up on whatever he wanted to try.

"So here's how it shapes up," Orrin said. "We want the money that was on the plane. We don't have time or inclination to sweet talk it out of you. You understand? If you want to walk out of this alive, hand it over."

"There was no money on the plane," Will said without hesitation.

And Taylor thought Will had called it right. No matter what they said or did, these bandits had no intention of letting them walk away alive.

"It's your funeral." Orrin nodded at the woman, who tightened her finger on the trigger. The blast tore through the night—drowning out Taylor's scream of protest—but amazingly Will was standing there, shocked and furious but still unharmed.

And Taylor, who had jumped forward instinctively, stopped dead, sick with relief—not even hearing Orrin's grim, "Don't do it, son!" Not noticing the semiautomatic aimed at him.

Stitch was poking his head out of the tent. He held Taylor's SIG. "Hey, look at this." He smiled a big, goofy smile. "Sweet!" He shoved the pistol into his belt, and crawled out of the tent. "There's nothing in there."

He picked up Will's backpack and began to go through it.

"The next one goes through your belly," Orrin said to Will. "It's your choice."

"There was no money," Taylor said desperately, and his fear for Will lent his tone a certain credibility that sounded misleadingly like truth.

"Maybe someone else took your money," Will said. "You ever think about that?"

Which was about as close as he could come to reminding them of their own missing confederate. Not that they would have forgotten, but they obviously weren't convinced of the way the skyjacking had gone, so they were eliminating possibilities. Taylor could follow their logic. And of course, while they couldn't know it, they were quite right about Will and himself—if for all the wrong reasons.

But then, that was the confusing thing: how couldn't they know it? How had they missed the body in the meadow? Or had they?

Yes, they had to have missed it, because if they'd found the body, there wouldn't be any question about who had that money—and Taylor knew they were uncertain. Not that their uncertainty would keep them from clipping either himself or Will—but he didn't let himself dwell on that.

If they'd been watching him and Will in the hot spring through binoculars they could have been miles back—still on the mountainside—which would have left them crossing that meadow in the dusk.

That was the only thing that made sense because if they'd been close enough to see them in the meadow, they'd have surely seen them stashing Taylor's pack in the bear box. And they wouldn't all be enjoying this little get-together.

"No money," Stitch said disgustedly, pulling Will's SIG P228 out of his backpack. He stuck that into his waistband too, and then turned the pack upside down, dumping all the packs of freeze-dried meals and desserts into the grass. "They got a helluva lotta food, that's for sure."

Silence.

"That *is* a lot of cheesecake," Orrin drawled thoughtfully. "I think maybe I'm inclined to believe you," he said to Taylor.

And Taylor knew Orrin was going to kill them.

Will must have drawn the same conclusion at the same instant. He said, "You're out of your fucking mind if you think you can murder two federal officers in cold blood and walk away."

Orrin said, "You'd be surprised at what people walk away with—when they're willing to take a few chances."

Now there was irony, and he hoped Will appreciated it; Taylor was pretty damn sure Orrin was a cop. The way he spoke, the way he handled himself: it all spelled law enforcement—maybe retired, given his age.

Will opened his mouth, and Taylor knew he was going to try and use the money as a bargaining chip. Waste of time. Any way you looked at it, they didn't need both him and Will, and they could ensure that the one left alive started talking just by blowing off a kneecap.

Orrin confirmed this the next moment by saying coolly, "All the same, I think we'll hang on to one of you for insurance. Just in case."

He looked from one to the other of them, and reading that expression, Taylor went for him. Because if it was coming down to him or Will, it had to be Will. Taylor couldn't see Will die and go on living. It was that simple.

But Stitch was there first, tackling him around the waist and throwing him back a few feet into the grass and weeds. Taylor landed awkwardly, only making it halfway to his feet before Stitch landed on him. It was like having a piano dropped on his chest, but it didn't matter; he already knew this was a lost cause. The point was to make the choice easy for Orrin—and to go down fighting—but as he delivered a few satisfying punches to Stitch's head, sending his hat flying, it occurred to Taylor to roll away from the campsite, to move toward the cliffside.

It was more instinct than sense, but he rolled again, managing to flip Stitch with him, and Stitch kept the momentum going, slugging in raw fury at Taylor. Somewhere in the background—behind Stitch's cursing and grunts—Taylor could hear Orrin shouting at them, and the woman's shrill tones.

And then a rifle butt slammed into his head, and all the fight drained out of him. Through the sick pain he could see Orrin standing over him, ready to strike again. And through the blur of tears and blood he saw Will edging forward, crowding the woman. She backed up, yelling for Orrin, bringing her rifle up to fire.

Orrin stepped away and turned his own rifle back on Will, who stopped in his tracks.

Stitch scrambled up, grabbed Taylor's jacket collar, dragging him to his knees. The barrel of his gun knocked against Taylor's face. He didn't care, didn't notice, all his focus on Orrin.

Orrin stared at Will. It felt like forever before he nodded at Taylor. "Yeah. He'd be less trouble. Kill him."

"Well, that doesn't make sense," the woman objected. "Why don't we kill *him*?" She nodded at Will, who stared stonily back at her.

Orrin said reasonably, "Because if you kill *him*, you'll have to kill pretty boy anyway. And we need to hang on to one of them in case we need a hostage."

Taylor heard his death sentence with something like relief, just making out the words over his own pained gulps for air and the distant thunder of the river crashing over the boulders down the mountainside behind them.

The woman and Stitch began to debate Orrin's decision. Taylor brought his head up for one last look at Will.

"My God, do I have to do everything myself?" Orrin inquired rhetorically, and the bullet slammed into Taylor's chest, left side—for a change—knocking him back. He went with it, letting himself topple right over the side of the mountain.

He nearly blacked out with the pain.

He slid and slithered a few feet, stones showering down around him, the momentum of his fall carrying him several yards down the slope. He rolled, trying to protect his head from trees and boulders, trying to absorb how badly he'd been hit, listening to the sound of the shot reverberating off the mountains—and the echo of Will's cry.

Will sounded... There were no words to describe that cry. Horror, grief—he'd sounded mortally wounded.

And after that one outcry, he sounded mad enough to kill—beyond rage, beyond sanity. Taylor, snatching frantically for handholds, anything to slow his descent, could hear him over the roar of the river below, ranting, swearing, threatening.

And then silence.

Jesus. Jesus, Will…

Let him be okay. Don't let them have changed their minds, don't let them have killed him…

He managed to grab onto a tangle of tree roots. A boulder, loosened by his brush against it, crashed on down the slope and plunged into the tumbling water below with a loud splash.

There had been no second shot, right? He hadn't heard a second shot.

The vegetation he was holding on to loosened in the wet soil above him, and Taylor refocused on his own peril: legs dangling over an outcrop of rocks and nothing but the cold night air and a couple hundred feet of falling beneath him. He shifted his grip, hauled himself up a foot, onto firmer ground. Dug his fingers and boot tips into the soggy earth.

He could hear voices drifting above him.

"He went into the river," Stitch called. "I heard his body hit the water."

Taylor, a couple of yards to the left, jammed his face into his arm and smothered his whimpers in his coat sleeve. He had to stay motionless, had to stay quiet, but the pain from being shot—again—was stupefying. Almost impossible to get beyond it.

But after a few moments of relative calm—of no longer falling down the slope and no more rocks raining down on him—and no more shooting at him—he did manage to think; and he began to wonder why he wasn't soaked in blood. There had been a hell of a lot of blood the other time; his body had begun to shut down immediately. That wasn't happening. Excruciating though the pain was, it was just…pain.

He reached up, feeling the hole in his jacket. He poked his finger through the leather, felt the hole in his shirt pocket—and there was dampness there, but not nearly enough—and then his fingertip touched metal. Dented metal. The stainless steel of Will's flask gently leaking bourbon around the lodged bullet in its face.

And for one crazy moment he almost laughed.

Jesus Christ. Saved by the bourbon. He struggled against the hysterical giggles threatening to burst out of his throat. It wasn't that funny, for God's sake, and he was still in a hell of a lot of trouble, but the relief of not being really shot again outweighed the extreme pain of being...well, shot again.

Let's hear a round of applause for the man upstairs...

He pulled himself up a few inches, trying for a more secure position, then rested, gathering himself, listening for what was happening topside. He couldn't hear much over the river's boom. But then he heard voices—and froze.

He knew that Stitch had been joined by the others, that they were all looking over the edge of the cliff, trying to spot his body in the water below—or on the slope.

He could just make out snatches of their discussion.

"He went in the river...splash was too heavy to be anything else..."

"What's that? There on the left?"

He stopped breathing, waiting, eyes staring into the darkness. He could just make out the dim outline of figures on the ledge above him but the moon was behind them, acting like a spotlight. He, on the other hand, lay in the deep shadows of the hillside. He could barely see his arm curled an inch or so in front of his nose.

Someone turned a flashlight on. The circle of light picked out a fallen tree, moved slowly across the hillside toward him...

He lay very still, trying not to breathe, praying the darkness and the scraggly vegetation concealed him. Every shallow, bruised breath was a reminder of how vulnerable he was, and the terror of being shot again was paralyzing—it hadn't been so bad when he didn't have time to think about it, but he was thinking about it now, thinking that he'd already had two close calls, and a third time was liable to be seriously unlucky. For the first time in his life he was too scared to move.

Fuck.

Please God…

"I'm telling you, he went in the river. I heard him hit the water."

"I don't see any blood." That was the woman. Taylor felt a surge of hatred for her. Why couldn't she mind her own business? Busybody bitch.

The flashlight beam swept past his boots and he tensed.

"Even if Orrin missed, there's no way he survived that drop."

"I'm just wondering why there's no blood."

And from further away: "That was point-blank range. One way or the other, he's history."

He couldn't hear Will. But then Will wouldn't have a lot to say now. Will was smart. Will knew when to shut up and what to do to stay alive. Will would be okay.

The flashlight switched off. The figures at the top of the hillside drew back.

Taylor closed his eyes. His chest hurt like he'd been kicked by a mule. Or a Transformer. He'd bought his nephew a couple of those for his birthday last week. Yeah, one of those red-eyed evil autobot dudes like Megatron or Starscream.

"If the river carries his body down…"

"…no ID on the body…"

Their voices were moving off.

A few moments later he nearly gave himself away when a couple of heavy items went smashing down the hillside past him—and he realized they had thrown Will's pack and the tent into the river.

CHAPTER SIX

"I *didn't even want to come on this goddamned trip. I did it for you."*

Taylor was dead. And he'd stood there and let it happen. Will felt dead himself; numb, empty—words didn't begin to cover it.

Taylor was dead. Confirming the almost superstitious dread that Will had felt for weeks—ever since Taylor had been hit—that they were on borrowed time, that Taylor's recovery had been nothing more than a temporary reprieve, that he had lost Taylor the night he'd turned him down. Told him he didn't love him.

Didn't love him?

And now it was too late.

"Are we going to walk all night?" the blond ape inquired. "Aren't we ever going to make camp?"

Orrin walked ahead carrying a high-powered flashlight, the beam catching stark glimpses of tree trunks, rocks, the crooked trail winding up through the hillside. Will's boot caught on a tree root; he stumbled over a rivulet in the trail, but caught himself.

"Don't even think about it, asshole." The woman nudged the base of Will's spine with the barrel of her rifle. He ignored her. He didn't give a damn if they shot him now. He should have jumped them when they killed Taylor. Why hadn't he? Why had he stood there? Why had he let the rifle pointed at his head stop him? What was wrong with him that he'd chosen to stay alive when they'd killed Taylor? Because Taylor wouldn't have; the gray-haired fucker had that right. Taylor would have gone for them; they'd have had to put him down to stop him. Taylor would have rather died—and so would Will, but yet Will had let them knock him down and tie his hands. He'd let them kill Taylor.

But what he wouldn't do was let them get away with it.

They were going to pay. He was going to stay alive that long. All three of them were going to pay—he wasn't sure how yet—for murdering Taylor. His eyes rested on Orrin's back, picturing with grim pleasure blowing a hole in its retreat.

"Hey, he's carrying a map or something in his pocket," Stitch reported suddenly. He reached forward and grabbed the map out of Will's back pocket.

Their weary procession stopped. Orrin plucked the map out of Stitch's hands, unfolding it and turning the flashlight on it.

"How'd you miss that, Bonnie?" Stitch said, and the woman's face—gargoyle-like in the ring of flashlights—twisted into a sneer.

"I had other things on my mind, moron. Like the fact that he's a goddamned fed!"

"Knock it off, you two." That was Orrin. He looked at Will and then down at the map. "Well, well. What's this?" He pointed at the circled point on the map.

Will stared at him without speaking.

Bonnie and Stitch glared at him. Orrin smiled. He had nice, even white teeth. "This is where the plane went down." The circle of flashlight beam moved across the map to the second circled point. "So what's so important here?"

"Figure it out," Will said.

"Oh, we will," Orrin said. "We will." He nodded to the others, and Bonnie prodded Will with her rifle again.

* * * * *

It had to be true love. Because if Taylor's only incentive for getting himself off that mountainside was his own health and welfare, he'd have been happy to spend the rest of his—few—days right where he was. But Will's only hope was Taylor, so he tried to work up a little enthusiasm.

But for chrissake...he'd already put in a full day's hike before he'd got punched a few times, got slammed in the head with a rifle butt, got shot, and then dived off a cliff. And lying here in the cold earth with a gentle mist coming down wasn't helping his recovery time.

On the positive side, he wasn't afraid of heights, and that was very good because when he looked down and saw nothing beneath him but the tumbling shine of the river and the swaying treetops, he felt a little...tired.

After all, technically he was still convalescent.

And while that bullet hadn't penetrated anything more vital than Will's flask, the impact had left bruises and contusions down the left side of his chest. The pain was draining, especially once the adrenaline that had numbed him to the worst of it faded away during the long, long minutes while he waited for the bandits to leave.

Even once he was sure it was safe to move, it was difficult to force himself to action. If he hadn't been afraid he'd fall off the mountainside he'd have closed his eyes for a few moments. As it was, he began to inch his way up, groping for handholds, feeling for something to brace his feet on.

The recent rains made it worse, causing the soft ground to slide out from under him, for plants to pull out by their roots when he tugged on them. It was slow—and nerve-wracking—going.

It took him forty-five minutes to crawl six yards, and by then Taylor was beginning to panic about Will. He was not going to be able to track these assholes through the woods; he couldn't afford to let them get too far ahead of him. He wasn't sure how long they planned on keeping Will alive. He wasn't sure why they felt they might need a hostage.

There was no guarantee that his worst nightmare wasn't waiting for him at the top—but he couldn't let himself think like that or he might as well let go and drop into the river.

He continued on his wet and muddy way, clambering up a few inches at a time, refusing to look down—and eventually refusing to look beyond his next handhold because his progress was too demoralizing. But then, finally, he was dragging himself over the embankment, lungs burning, muscles screaming, body soaked in sweat. He crawled away from the edge, scanning the now empty campsite, verifying—and re-verifying—that Will was not lying there dead. He let himself collapse, resting his head on his forearms, closing his eyes.

His heart was racketing around his chest like it was trying to find an escape route.

He only allowed himself a few minutes before he pushed up and began trying to figure which way Orrin and his pals had taken Will. It would have been nice if Will had left some sign or some clue, but Will, of course, believed Taylor was dead.

At first studying the ground seemed hopeless. As far as Taylor was concerned a herd of wildebeests could have been milling around the clearing, but after a time the moon rose above the trees and he began to discern the mess of footprints into separate tracks.

They were using the trail heading back toward the meadow and lake, retracing the path that Will and Taylor had taken that afternoon. Obviously they weren't worried about being followed—or even running into other hikers or park rangers.

Every so often Taylor got a faraway glimpse of light through the trees—the stray beam of a flashlight. And once he heard the sharp clatter of rock on rock—miles ahead and outdistancing him fast.

He didn't allow himself to think about anything but getting to Will in time. If he stopped to consider his own situation…well, forgetting about his various aches and pains for a moment—which wasn't all that easy to do the longer the night wore on—he'd never felt quite this isolated or lost. Not in any of his foreign postings, but then he'd never been so far out of his own element.

Not even in an Afghan embassy compound surrounded by a desert full of hostiles.

He wasn't sure how long he followed Orrin and the others, but he was headed back through one of the meadows he and Will had crossed earlier that day when he saw motion in the darkness ahead.

Not far enough ahead, unfortunately—as an indescribable heavy oily scent of wet fur, fish, and grass resolved itself into an enormous black bulk that suddenly rose up on its hind legs.

A bear.

Taylor stopped dead, hand reaching automatically for his shoulder holster—which was not there.

The bear, a weaving shadow in the darkness, made a heavy blowing out sound and then a strange wooden clicking noise.

Jesus. What was he supposed to do—besides not run? That much he knew. You didn't run from a bear. And you didn't try to climb a tree. What the hell had Will said about this? Play dead with grizzlies and fight back with black bears. And there were no grizzlies in the High Sierras so…yell, make noise, clap hands—and if he started yelling and screaming he was liable to alert Orrin and his pals that he was alive and on their trail.

Taylor took a careful sliding step backward. The bear was still blowing and making those clacking sounds. It had to be six feet tall and about three hundred pounds. It looked like it was all claws and teeth to Taylor.

Funny. They looked so cute in the zoo.

"Get the hell out of here, you sonofabitch," Taylor growled, trying to look and sound aggressive. He bent down, hands skittering over pine cones, rejecting them—he didn't want to merely annoy the thing—and caught up a stone, pelting it hard at the bear. It bounced off its head. The bear made more exhalations and chomping sounds, and Taylor, scrabbling for more stones, wasn't sure if he was merely pissing it off. He pitched another couple of hard balls—putting everything he had into his throw—and to his relief the bear dropped back on all fours and lumbered away, crashing through the brush and bushes.

For a few seconds Taylor stood there panting; he hadn't thought he had that much adrenaline left. He mopped his wet fore-head with his sleeve.

"I *hate* camping," he said softly, just for the record.

* * * * *

He was weaving with exhaustion when he gave in to the need for sleep. Even after he decided to rest, it took him time to find a safe and suitable place. Safe and suitable being relative. Finally he took shelter in a small cavity in the hillside. It wasn't large or deep enough to be a cave, but that was fine by Taylor. A cave was likely to be already inhabited, and he'd had all the close encounters with local wildlife he could handle for one night. He tucked himself in the little vault made by a couple of precariously balanced boulders, huddling, arms wrapped around his bent knees, head resting on folded arms. The rocks weren't warm, but they protected him from the wind and the night air, and at least it was relatively dry.

He closed his eyes.

The night seemed alive with sound. Far noisier than the city ever had.

He let himself dream of Will. Only half dream really—and half confused memory. Memories of when they had first been part-nered. Nothing dramatic. Not like TV shows where the partners hate each other on sight but then come to like and eventually trust each other. The fact was, he'd liked Will right away. Liked his se-riousness, his professionalism. Will was relaxed and experienced, and his calm approach to the job was a good balance for Taylor's own more...intense work style. He'd liked Will's sense of humor, and when he'd realized Will was gay...

For the first time ever in DSS he'd felt completely at ease, completely comfortable…understood and appreciated. Up until this week, he couldn't have conceived of voluntarily seeking another partner.

He tried to picture that: getting used to someone who wasn't Will. Maybe someone who took his coffee black, who didn't like overpriced bourbon or dumb action films, who dated girls from the Computer Investigations Branch, and didn't own a beer-drinking dog or listen to Emmylou Harris. Someone who wasn't allergic to penicillin or who wasn't an expert marksman. Someone who might not be there the next time he got his ass into a jam.

He thought of waking up in the hospital with Will sitting right there. His eyes had been bluer than summer skies, and his smile had been sort of quizzical. "Welcome back," he'd said in that gentle voice he'd used for the first few days after Taylor recovered consciousness. And Taylor had managed a smile because it was Will—despite the fact that he'd never been in so much pain in his entire life.

And all the other times Will had shown up bearing magazines and fruit and CDs—sometimes only managing to squeak in about five minutes before visiting hours were over.

A million memories. A million moments. Will's laugh, the way his eyes tilted when he was teasing, the way he bit his lip when he was worried, that discreet tattoo of a griffin on his right shoulder—the way his skin had tasted this afternoon. The way his mouth had tasted…

* * * * *

It was still dark when Taylor woke. He was freezing. He was starving. He could hear the high-pitched yapping hysteria of coyotes. They sounded close by. Too close. But he knew enough to know it was unlikely coyotes were going to attack a full-grown man. He pressed the dial of his wristwatch and studied the luminous face. Two-thirty in the morning. Still a couple of hours of darkness. He needed to get moving again.

But as he crawled outside his shelter, he was seized with doubt. Was he making a mistake following Will and his captors? What if he couldn't catch up with them in time? He had no idea how long they would keep Will alive. Would the smarter move be to go for help? Get off the mountain and get down to the nearest ranger station?

For a moment he was torn. If he got this wrong, it meant Will's life.

* * * * *

"So what was it? You didn't like the retirement package?" Will asked conversationally as Orrin settled across from him, rifle across his lap, when they finally stopped for the night.

"Can we have a fire?" Bonnie asked.

"Nope. We don't want to attract any more goddamn rangers." Then Orrin nodded at Will as though acknowledging a point scored. "Yeah, it's always the quiet ones you've got to watch. I pegged you for trouble right off the bat."

Will ignored that. He wasn't going to be distracted by the pain of remembering Orrin playing God. He couldn't let himself think about Taylor, couldn't let himself grieve until he'd done what he needed to do—starting with surviving this night.

"You're a cop?"

"Deputy sheriff. Used to be." Orrin watched Bonnie huddling down in her sleeping bag. Just for a moment something softened in his weathered face. Bonnie didn't fit Will's idea of a femme fatale, but to each his own.

"Let me guess. The line got blurry watching all those bad guys get away with it year after year," he mocked.

Orrin shrugged genially. "Something like that. Anyway, it's not like we robbed a mom and pop store. We hit a casino."

"And killed two sheriff's deputies and the pilot of the plane you hijacked."

"And your partner," Orrin said evenly.

Will said very quietly, "And my partner."

For a moment Orrin's gaze held his. He said softly, "You're not going to get the chance, son."

Will smiled—and had the satisfaction of seeing Orrin's eyes narrow.

"Was it really just a coincidence you were up here?" Bonnie asked suddenly, opening her eyes.

Will turned his head her way. She had a hard, plain face, drab blonde hair. Maybe she looked different when she wasn't cold, miserable, and had fixed herself up, put a little makeup on. Or maybe she had nothing to do with it; maybe she was just one of the perks for Orrin.

"It was just a coincidence," he replied.

"I don't believe in coincidence," she said. "I don't even believe in luck."

"The house always wins?" Will said.

"That's right."

"Stop jabbering and let me get to sleep," Stitch complained, lying a few feet away.

Will stared across at Orrin. Orrin stared back.

* * * * *

He thought about the days after Taylor had been shot—days spent prowling Little Saigon looking for the two punks that the restaurant owner next door had seen screeching away from the parking lot behind the nail salon.

With the help of the Orange County Sheriff's Department he'd tracked Daniel Nguyen and Le Loi Roy to their favorite noodle shop where the teenage gangstas were scarfing down pigskin-filled rice paper wraps. Nguyen had surrendered without trouble, but Le Loi Roy had gone for a shoot-out at the bok choy corral and wound up with a shattered hip and a couple of missing fingers. He was fifteen. Nguyen was thirteen.

When questioned about the nail salon incident, according to Nguyen, the FBI guy—who was Taylor, apparently—had drawn his gun but had hesitated—and Le Loi had shot him. To Nguyen's way of looking at it that made it self-defense.

Le Loi's story—when he was well enough to offer one—was that the FBI guy had waited too long—obviously thinking they were a couple of dumb little kids. Too bad for him. Le Loi had been chagrined to hear that he had not actually killed the FBI guy as this was seriously going to damage his own newly-minted street cred.

The couple of times Will had tried to talk to Taylor about it, Taylor claimed he didn't remember much of anything. He didn't want to discuss it—didn't want to hear about the fate of Daniel Nguyen and Le Loi Roy, and Will – reprimanded and removed from the case himself—let it drop. The trial was scheduled for May, still two months away. Moot now with Taylor dead.

* * * * *

Once, Will thought Orrin might just be drifting toward sleep, but he sat up, shifting the rifle abruptly, and pinning his gaze on Will's watchful face.

"If I were you, son, I'd grab some shut-eye."

"You're not me," Will said pleasantly. "And I'm not your son."

Orrin laughed. Glanced at his confederates, who were soundly sleeping. Stitch's snores were loud enough to echo off the mountains.

"What was his name? Your partner."

"MacAllister. Taylor MacAllister."

"Partners a long time?"

"Four years in June."

"That's a long time in law enforcement. How'd that work? You and him being…?" Orrin made a seesawing hand gesture.

Will opened his mouth and then recognized that sorrowful inevitable truth for what it was, and changed what he had been about to say. "It worked fine till you killed him."

"I had a partner for a few years. Meanest sonofabitch you'd ever want to meet."

"That's quite a compliment coming from you," Will said.

Orrin laughed. Then he called to Bonnie and Stitch. They came awake immediately, rolling over and sitting up. Will noted that Bonnie reached for her rifle first thing. Stitch went for his boots. Good to know.

"Orrin, can we please have a fire? I'm freezing my butt off," Bonnie complained through chattering teeth, pulling her boots on.

"Yeah. Stitch, collect some firewood and we'll have some coffee and breakfast. We got a long day ahead of us." Orrin pulled out Will's map and studied it by the light of his flashlight.

"How long are we —?" Bonnie nodded toward Will.

"We'll see how useful he makes himself," Orrin replied.

"I've gotta pee," Bonnie announced, and wandered off into the bushes.

She wandered back a short time later and took Orrin's place while Orrin vanished to relieve himself. He left his rifle propped against a rock, but Will knew he was carrying Taylor's SIG. He had taken it from Stitch; spoils of war, apparently. All the same, this was probably as good a chance as he was going to get. He studied Bonnie. Rifle aimed at him, she stood poised and ready for him to try something—dangerous with nerves and fatigue.

"Quit staring at me," she said shortly, though it was too dark for either of them to really see what the other was looking at.

"It's not too late to get yourself out of this," Will said. "You're not the one who shot a federal agent. If you help me —"

"Orrin!" she yelled.

Orrin came back fast, zipping up his pants. "What's going on?"

"He's trying to work me! He's going to try and play us off against each other!"

"Of course he is," Orrin said reasonably. "Wouldn't you?"

"Yeah, well, it just might work on that moron Stitch."

"Where *is* Stitch?" Orrin said abruptly, looking around the clearing.

"He's gathering wood for the fire," Bonnie said.

"We're not building a bonfire, for God's sake." Orrin walked out a little way, yelling for Stitch.

The silence that followed his call was eerie.

"Stitch!" shrieked Bonnie. Her voice seemed to echo off the distant mountains and come rolling back louder than before.

Orrin shushed her impatiently. They listened intently. "Okay, keep an eye on him." He added as Will moved to stand up, "No, you don't. Stay where you are, son."

"No!" Bonnie said. "We need to stay together."

A tall shadow stepped out of the trees: Orrin's flashlight gleamed off the rifle barrel pointed straight at him.

"Together is good," Taylor said.

CHAPTER SEVEN

For one very strange moment Will thought he might—for the first time in his entire life—faint. He could actually hear the blood surging in his head, drowning out coherent thought. The shock was enough to send him rocking back on his heels, staring in disbelief at the slender shadow that resolved itself into a tense and familiar outline.

"Where's Stitch?" Orrin asked evenly, gaze on the rifle Taylor held. And aside from that pregnant pause before he spoke, he seemed to take Taylor's return from the dead without batting an eyelash.

"Unavailable."

Taylor's voice. Taylor. Alive.

Taylor said, "Will?"

"Right here."

"Are you okay?"

"I am now."

Orrin chuckled, and the sound was jarring. "Son, you can't take both of us. Even if you do shoot me before I get to my rifle —"

"He's got your SIG," Will interrupted.

Orrin chuckled again. "Even if you did hit me at this distance and in this light, Bonnie will blow a hole through lover boy over there. No way you can take us both in time."

"You're right," Taylor said. "But I guarantee I can—and will—take *you*." And they could all hear the easy confidence in his voice.

Bonnie was shaking, but she knew better than to take her eyes off Will for one second. "Orrin?" she said worriedly.

Orrin didn't say anything, his hand still resting on the rifle stock, but making no move to pick it up.

"All it takes is one .22 plowing right between your eyes and into that lizard brain of yours, and that's it for you, Orrin," Taylor said. "I won't make the same mistake you did."

"Okay," Orrin said. "So what do you think you have to bargain with?"

"Your life." Taylor barely tilted his head in Will's direction. "The only reason you're not already dead is I want him."

"You do seem sorta sweet on each other," Orrin remarked. He barely twitched his fingers and Taylor took two fast steps forward, his finger caressing the trigger but somehow managing not to pull. "Okay, okay. Keep your hair on!" Orrin said, holding very still. "So what's your plan, son? Him for me, is that the deal?"

"That's the deal."

The inability to read anyone's face made the moment all the more fraught. Taylor's outline was poised, ready. But despite his hard calm, Will felt his tension, and he suddenly knew what Taylor was afraid of. Stitch must not be dead, and wherever he was, Taylor was afraid he wasn't going to stay there long enough.

"Mexican standoff." Orrin sounded amused.

The woman said, "Orrin…" as Will used his back against the tree trunk behind him to lever to his feet. He took a slow step away from her, aiming for the shadows of the trees.

His hands were still tied behind his back, which meant he was going to have trouble running. But they needed to go because the minute Stitch turned up, armed or unarmed, the balance tipped out of their favor.

Will passed Taylor, reaching the fingertips of the shadows. Taylor took a slow, careful step backward, his bead on Orrin never wavering.

"Orrin —" Bonnie moved, trying to keep Will in her sights

"It's okay," Orin said calmly. "They're not going far."

Will reached the safety of the thicket, and a moment later Taylor was beside him—and a moment after that Bonnie and Orrin opened fire.

Taylor dived to the side, taking Will with him. The air was alive with gunfire, and they stayed low, moving fast, plastered to the ground as they crawled for cover. Or Taylor crawled. With his hands behind his back, Will was reduced to trying to hump along with Taylor tugging at him, half-dragging him.

They weren't going to get far like this, but apparently Taylor wasn't trying to get far, just get them into concealment. They plowed right into a stand of thick vegetation, flattening themselves to the ground. Will opened his mouth to ask what Taylor had in mind, but Taylor reached out and scooped up some wet earth, smearing it over Will's face. The cold of the mud silenced Will. He watched Taylor camouflage his own face.

The shooting had stopped and the silence was nerve-wrenching.

Bushes rustled noisily down the path. A tall shadow staggered drunkenly out of the trees. Taylor breathed an obscenity. Before Will had a chance to work it out, he spotted muzzle flash to the left. A rifle opened fire and the second rifle joined in a moment later. There was an animal scream as bullets tore apart the shrubs and low-hanging tree limbs.

Will tried to get lower, but molded to the ground was about as low as it got.

Silence. They could hear Bonnie and Orrin thrashing about in the bushes.

"Oh my God," screeched the woman. "It's Stitch!"

Will picked up the lower murmur of Orrin speaking too, but his voice didn't carry as well.

"Well, what was he *doing* here?"

More muted words from Orrin.

"Christ," Will breathed. He glanced at Taylor. He could only make out the shine of his eyes.

"I thought I hit him harder than that," Taylor said almost inaudibly. He didn't seem particularly distressed as he glanced at Will. "One down, two to go," and Will saw the glimmer of his smile.

Abruptly, Orrin and Bonnie started firing again, startling Taylor into immobility. A lot of firepower raking through the brush—you had to respect that—but the shooting seemed to be moving in the wrong direction—away from them, and it began to seem that Orrin and Bonnie were just taking their frustrations out in ammo.

Taylor cracked open the barrel of the .22, checked the magazine and swore very softly. "Three cartridges," he mouthed to Will.

Not good.

Under the barrage of rifle shots, Taylor nudged Will back into motion, guiding him with one hand locked on his arm. They wove their way through the ferns and bushes, hunched down, stopping every few feet to listen.

Taylor pulled him down, and Will knelt, trying not to lose his balance. Taylor's hands felt over him, covering Will's for a fleeting moment, as Taylor groped for the cords binding his wrists. Will could hear the grin in his whispered, "So…did you miss me?"

"I thought you were dead," Will said simply. He couldn't joke, couldn't cover, couldn't pretend it had been anything but what it seemed: the end of everything he cared about—made all the worse by the realization that he hadn't accepted how important Taylor was to him until it was too late.

Taylor said calmly, "Yeah, sorry about that." And from his tone Will knew that Taylor at least partly understood what he wasn't saying. "Are you okay? They didn't rough you up too much?"

For a minute Will couldn't manage his voice. "You shouldn't have come back for me," he got out finally.

"You have the car keys." Taylor was working the knots frantically. Thin, strong fingers wriggling and tugging—apparently without luck. *"Fuck."*

"I can run like this if I have to," he reassured softly.

Bullshit with which Taylor didn't even bother to argue.

He did more picking and pulling and plucking and prying, and finally Will felt the cords around his wrists loosen and fall away. He shook his hands free, and Taylor grabbed up the rope and stuffed it into his jacket pocket, which was good thinking since it was hard to know what might come in handy later.

Clenching his jaw against the torture of blood rushing back into his arms and fingers, Will was dimly aware of Taylor's hands rubbing, trying to aid circulation. He was astonished when Taylor suddenly pulled him into his arms, lowering his head to Will's. For a moment he was held fiercely. He felt Taylor's lips graze his cheekbone, and then Taylor had let him go again, turned away.

Will yanked him back, running his hands over him until he found the bullet hole in his jacket.

"I knew it. You *were* hit." His probing fingers found the punctured flask. "Taylor… Christ."

"It's okay. I'm fine. A couple of bruises." And he freed himself, crawling out of the thicket, moving slowly, stealthily. Will followed—shaky with an emotion that had nothing to do with their peril or the pain in his arms and hands.

Since Taylor now seemed to have a plan, Will kept silent until they found the place where the trail branched off.

In the opposite direction they could hear the crack of sticks and twigs, the echo of voices. Every so often a light flashed through the trees.

"It's not going to take them long to figure out we doubled back," he warned.

Taylor nodded, and started down the sharply descending path.

The crack of a rifle split the night.

The echo ringing off the mountains made it hard to judge direction. It was possible that they had been spotted, or that Orrin and company were shooting at something else.

To the left there was a clatter of falling stones, a small slide maybe—hard to identify in the darkness. Taylor started running—Will right on his heels.

They sprinted down the crooked trail like deer outracing brush fire, flying—sometimes literally—over the dips and rocks and fallen tree limbs, feet pounding the muddy trail. Taylor slithered once, and Will's hand shot out, steadying him. Will tripped a few yards further on and Taylor grabbed him by the collar before he went tumbling. Both times they barely slowed their headlong rush.

The miracle was they didn't break their necks or at the least a leg in the first three minutes. The stars were fading in the sky but there was no light to speak of, and even if there had been, the trail was mostly in the shadow of the mountainside, which was to their advantage in one way—and not at all in another.

But it had a kind of amusement park ride charm to it, Will thought vaguely, barely catching himself from turning into a human avalanche yet again. That time he saved himself by jumping and landing, still running, on the trail winding below.

Somehow they made it down to the bottom without killing themselves. Taylor dropped down on all fours, gulping for air. Will walked a loose circle, giving his burning muscles a chance to recover, trying to catch his breath, listening for sounds of chase.

Throwing a look at the face of the craggy mountainside just beginning to materialize in the dawn, he was belatedly stricken at what they had attempted. It was a good thing he hadn't realized it before they started running.

At muffled sounds of distress, he turned his head. Next to a small rivulet splashing down into a rocky pool, Taylor was on his knees, being quietly sick. Will didn't blame him. That trail had to have dropped five hundred feet in less than a mile. Will thought he might have left his own stomach somewhere around the last bend.

Kneeling, Will put a hand on his shoulder. "You okay?"

Taylor nodded, scooped a hand in the water and splashed his face, further smearing the mud and sweat.

Will gave him a moment, rising and scanning the mountain-side for the flashlights, for motion, for anything indicating pursuit.

Nothing.

That didn't mean they weren't being followed. The tiny waterfall rushing down into the pool at the foot of the path effectively drowned out the most immediate of the night sounds.

"We've got to keep moving," he said, and Taylor nodded, got one knee under and shoved himself back to his feet.

They staggered their way down the canyon, finally taking shelter behind a series of sandy rock formations as the blackness of night began to dull to gray. From this vantage point they'd be able to see in all directions once it turned daylight. But once it turned daylight, they needed to be moving again. Will lay on his belly, watching.

There was nothing.

Taylor was on his back, his head leaning against the edge of Will's shoulder. Will listened to him struggle to catch his breath. He thought Taylor's inhalations sounded funky: sort of squeaky… wheezy; was the injured lung holding up to the strain?

"Okay?" he asked, undervoiced.

Taylor nodded. Then shook his head. "Need a…minute."

Yeah. They both needed a minute. But Taylor sounded winded. And Will could feel him shaking with exhaustion. Not that Will wasn't shaky himself, but he was in better shape than Taylor. He turned it over in his mind. He didn't like being on defense, but Taylor's fatigue made any kind of offense impossible for now.

Assuming Orrin and Bonnie didn't give up and go home—and he couldn't see how they could afford to do that—they'd expect him and Taylor to continue down to safety and civilization, and they'd attempt to cut them off. That's what he'd do in their position. Will shifted, and Taylor rolled away, swallowing hard.

"What do you want to do?" he whispered.

"We rest for a minute. Then we move to higher ground."

Taylor's face turned toward him. "We could split up. Make it harder for them."

"We're not splitting up." Will held Taylor's eyes with his own. "Never again."

Taylor laughed.

"Something funny?"

"The whole goddamned thing is funny." It sounded like he had recovered his breath, anyway. Will took care of that by covering Taylor's mouth with his own in a quick, hard kiss.

* * * * *

The sky was turning a peachy pink when they started up the slope, sticking to rock as much as possible in an effort to hide their tracks.

Without his map it was hard to be sure, but Will thought they were on the west side of Elk Pass. This was confirmed when they later came upon an old, half-tumbled down mining shack.

There had been no sign of any pursuit since they'd made their escape down the cliff the night before. Will thought they could risk going to ground for a few hours. It wasn't like they had a choice, really. Taylor was moving on willpower alone, and he needed time to figure out how they were going to get to help before Orrin and Bonnie got to them.

Will kicked the door, and half the wall fell in. Taylor began to laugh. And soft though it was, it echoed off the rocks and bounced around the canyon, a ghostly chuckle in the crisp, cold dawn.

"Shhh. *Shit,*" Will hissed, but he started to laugh too. "Be quiet, for God's sake." He grabbed Taylor and pushed him through the broken door—and wall—realizing how glad he was to have an excuse to hold him.

"Jesus, there could be snakes…spiders…" Taylor was letting Will guide him under the half-fallen logs which made a kind of lean-to. He got down on his hands and knees. "Are you sure this is safe?"

His muffled complaint nearly started Will laughing again.

"You mean is it up to code? Probably not." Will shoved him, not ungently, hands lingering. "Get in there."

And Taylor handed him the rifle and crawled the rest of the way beneath the makeshift shelter. He drew his long legs up, and Will wriggled in beside him. The smell of damp earth and moldering wood and leather and perspiration was warm and strangely reassuring. Taylor was scrunched up against him, shoulder to shoulder, hip to hip.

"Comfortable?" he asked, and Taylor started that wheezy laughing again. "Will you shut up?" But he couldn't get any heat into it.

After a few moments, Taylor quieted. "I don't see why they would come after us. It makes more sense for them to give up on the money and get out while they can."

Will didn't answer.

"Don't you think?"

"No," said Will. "And neither do you."

Taylor sighed and shifted. They sat for a time…listening.

Taylor's head dropped forward, and he jerked awake. He swore quietly.

Will whispered, "Put your head on my shoulder."

"I'm awake."

"Put your head on my shoulder. I'll take first watch."

There was something wary in Taylor's silence. At last, he adjusted position, lowering his head to Will's shoulder. They sat there stiffly for a moment or two, but then Taylor settled more comfortably; his breath was warm against Will's throat.

"Hold on," Will mumbled. He wriggled, got his arm free, and slid it around Taylor's back, pulling him close and offering a little more support. "You can stretch out if you want to."

"There's no room."

"Yeah, there is. Stretch out to the side of me." Will tried to shift more, and Taylor inched down a little. A board slid from above them, clattering loudly in the crisp morning.

They both froze. Then Will said grimly, "Careful. Don't knock down our happy home."

Taylor's laugh was a breath of sound, then he swore again, and Will guided him down the length of his own body, hands moving over Taylor's jean-clad legs, his hips, his torso. He just managed to avoid Taylor head-butting him, and then Taylor's hand landed on his crotch.

Will was a little surprised at his body's instant reaction, but that was adrenaline for you. His cock pressed uncomfortably against the canvas pants.

"Ow," Taylor said.

"Whaddya mean, 'ow'? You're the one doing all the banging."

There was an astonished silence, then Taylor muttered, his knee just missing a vital part of Will's expanding anatomy, "I'm pleading the fifth."

He finally got himself positioned to his satisfaction, the heat of his body pressed down the length of Will's, his head resting once more on Will's shoulder. He put his arm around Will's waist, and Will put his arm around Taylor's shoulders.

"Comfortable?" He was grinning, although there wasn't much to smile at.

"Oh, yeah. You didn't forget to put out the Do Not Disturb sign, did you?"

"Nah. And room service at seven."

Taylor expelled a long breath that sounded mostly like a moan.

Will patted him absently. Seconds later he could tell by Taylor's breathing he was asleep.

CHAPTER EIGHT

He came awake to shivery darkness, and he couldn't remember for a moment where he was or what had happened. But he was lying with someone—on the cold, very hard ground it seemed—and he was being undressed, warmed. Warm hands undoing his shirt, sliding inside and stroking him. Part caress, part reassurance, part…salvage effort. Comfort and joy—and he…knew those hands. Knew that touch.

He parted his lips and to his delight, a warm mouth covered his own. And he knew that taste too.

Taylor opened his eyes and Will was a warm bulk lying against him, Will's hands moved over him, and Will was undressed too, heated skin, soft hair, hot mouth licking Taylor's nipples into taut little points.

"We'll be warmer like this," he whispered.

Yes, it was definitely warmer like this. Taylor slipped his hands beneath Will's arms for a moment, enjoying being held, treasuring the flush of heat between them, his own shivers easing in the wake of excitement and pleasant sleepy surprise. He remembered now. Remembered where they were—and why—that waking up at all was a miracle, let alone waking up in each other's arms—which they most definitely were.

"Morning…"

Will's mouth found his own again—hungry, calescent—and traveled a slow, lazy trail down Taylor's jaw…throat…collarbone… gentling over the puckered scar on Taylor's chest. Taylor sucked in his breath.

"Does that hurt?"

He shook his head, although the scars were still sensitive, still felt weird being touched; he wouldn't want anyone to see them, let alone touch them—but it was different with Will.

This felt healing. The moist trace of lips, the delineation of tongue. He nipped Will's ear, and Will caught his breath, nudged Taylor's face, finding his mouth again for a hard, sweet kiss. A lover's kiss—while Will's fingertips dusted lightly over the whorls of damaged tissue. A little more to the left and the bullet would have hit Taylor's heart, but there it was thumping away, fast and strong against Will's fingertips, and desire buzzed through his nervous system, and he had never felt more alive than he felt right now.

Will's hands slid down, fastening on Taylor's waist, holding on, lips moving over Taylor's. Hot and soft, Will's tongue pushing inside Taylor's mouth, and Taylor mewled, wriggling closer.

The roughness of their jaws rubbing against each other, eyelashes flickering against each other, noses rubbing against each other.

Taylor tore his mouth away and said breathlessly, "You must not think we're going to make it."

"We're going to make it."

"Yeah? What's this supposed to be? A mercy fuck?" Taylor was smiling—he could feel Will's surprise.

Will shut him up the best way he knew, slipping his tongue back inside Taylor's mouth, teasing and sweet, playful like they had all the time in the world—like they should have done a long time ago.

Taylor's newly warmed hands slid eagerly over Will's body, moving to the fastening of his pants, and Will reciprocated, undoing Taylor's jeans and working his hand inside Taylor's boxers as they humped against each other, pressing close, hips grinding, cocks stiff and shoving against each other.

Palming one hard ass cheek, Will pinched. Taylor bucked. Will smoothed away the sting, smiling against Taylor's mouth, and their kiss went deeper, hotter, tongues twining.

Will thrust up, Taylor arched back, and they were struggling desperately to find the rhythm, pushing into each other's touch, frantic with need to be together in this, burning up with it.

Will was panting against his ear, hot moist gusts. Taylor pulled him closer, bit his throat, groaning pleasurably when Will nipped back. Bodies writhing, cocks rubbing, chests pushing against each other—it was feverish and fast and all too fleeting. Will reached down and took Taylor's wet-tipped cock in his hand, and Taylor rocked up against him, hands reaching up blindly, sliding down his biceps, hips pushing frantically into Will's grasp.

"You're purring again," Will said unsteadily, starting to laugh. "That is…beautiful…"

He was working both their cocks together, and Taylor struggled not to thrash around, to keep his movements tiny and tight because he didn't want to knock down the entire building. He fastened his mouth over Will's, smothering the yell he knew was coming.

And sure enough, Will's body bowed and then released in blazing hot pulse beats, slick heat spilling over Taylor's hand while he tried to hush Will's cries against his own.

Will shuddered all over, his hands faltering for a moment, going soft. He tore his mouth away, gasping for air. Taylor jerked against him, frustrated, and then Will's hands tightened again, and he set Taylor free with a couple of hard strokes, and bright release crackled through his body like raw electric current. He was coming hard, and he felt Will's hand slip, regain its grip, and milk him of the last sweet splashes of liquid heat.

They rested together then, warm and drowsy while the birds in the meadow sang good morning.

* * * * *

Will stroked Taylor's hair, fingering the little streak of silver that had appeared after the shooting. "It's light. We should get moving."

Taylor nodded. "They've got your map?"

"I don't think they'll go for the money now. They'll figure they have to stop us first."

"But they've gotta know they're running out of time. What are they going to do about Stitch's body?"

"There are all kinds of places they can stash that body. It could be months—years—before anyone discovers it."

"If it was me, I'd go for the money."

Will grinned reluctantly. "Yeah, but you've got nerves of steel. Nothing distracts you from what you want."

"You oughta talk," Taylor said. "Anyway, I've been known to...cut my losses." A little muscle moved in his jaw. "I know not everything I want is possible."

"What do you want?" Will asked. His fingers brushed Taylor's cheek, feeling the softness of beard over the hard planes of jaw. "Besides getting out of here alive."

Taylor didn't speak for a moment. "I want you," he said at last. Sunlight filtering through a chink in the lean-to illuminated his face. He looked tired and unexpectedly vulnerable. "I know what you think. And I know I don't have a great record when it comes to relationships, but —"

"Four years," Will interrupted. "Or close enough. That's how long we've been partners—that's the longest relationship I've ever had, and it's been with you."

To his surprise, Taylor's face quivered. He closed his eyes, hiding his feelings from Will, and Will absently noted how long his eyelashes were. He'd noticed that in the hospital too, sitting by Taylor's bedside waiting for him to wake up. Those long, black eyelashes…

"Hey," he said softly, "are you falling asleep in the middle of my big romantic speech?"

Taylor's lashes lifted. "Did you mean it? What you said before about taking it one day at a time?"

"Yeah, I meant it. Of course I did. I'm not letting you go without a fight."

Taylor said carefully, "As your partner or —?"

"As my friend, my lover, my partner. All of it. One day at a time," Will said. "Starting with today." And this time his kiss was a promise.

* * * * *

"Watch for rock slides here," Will warned.

It was late afternoon. It had taken the larger part of the day to cut back over the bluffs and they were working their way down the back of the mountainside. There was no trail to speak of, and they had to focus on their footing. Far below was a long valley with what appeared to be the scattered buildings of a ranch.

"What is that?" Taylor asked, sliding to a stop beside Will.

"I think that's the health resort I was telling you about." Will shaded his eyes, studying the empty corrals and tumbled down buildings. "It looks abandoned."

"We could burn the buildings down." And at Will's expression, Taylor said, "We've got to get the attention of someone: other hikers, rangers, campers. We can't keep this up forever."

Will's gaze was measuring, and Taylor said, "That's not what I mean. I'm okay, but we can't play hide and seek on this mountain all day."

"Yeah, you're great. We both are. Tired, hungry, thirsty —" He brushed the edge of his thumb against Taylor's cheekbone. "Sunburned. Next time, you pick the vacation spot."

"Now *that* I'm holding you to." Taylor smothered a yawn. "Maybe they did go after the money."

Will shook his head. "Even if they went to that meadow and found Jackson's body, they know we were there first. It's just going to confirm their suspicion that we found the money and hid it. And they're right."

"If they did use your map to find the meadow, how long would it take them?"

Will did some calculations. "If they started last night they'd have reached the meadow by midmorning."

"They'd look around to see if we hid the money. They were tracking us with binoculars from the time we stopped at the mineral springs."

"We'd already hidden the money by then—and if they knew where we'd stashed it, they wouldn't have bothered tracking us down last night."

"Do you think there's any chance they could follow our tracks to the bear box?"

"One of that group has a fair amount of tracking experience. I'm guessing it's Orrin." Will's eyes met Taylor's. "But I think they'll come straight after us. They know we eventually have to make our way down. They'll try to intercept."

"Then we better keep moving." Taylor rose and reached down a hand to Will.

* * * * *

The wind made a mournful sound through the broken boards of the old lodge. Shafts of sunlight, fading with the dimming daylight, highlighted floating motes—and striped the body lying facedown in the dust. The bullet hole in the back of the uniform jacket was crusted with blood several days old.

"Jesus." Taylor buried his nose in the crook of his arm as he approached the corpse. "That's why they thought they might need an insurance policy. They killed a ranger."

He glanced back; Will was standing in the open doorway watching the hills behind them.

"Everything okay?"

Will nodded—but absently. "I'm not sure. I thought I saw a flash on that hillside."

Taylor joined him and they watched for a moment.

Nothing moved. Nothing but the ripple of winter grass in the fields.

"Why hasn't anyone noticed they're missing a park ranger?"

Will shook his head. "Maybe they have." His eyes never left the pine-studded hillside.

"Are you thinking what I'm thinking?" Taylor asked.

Will turned his head and grinned slowly. "Probably."

* * * * *

"Actually, what I'm thinking is I'm going to have to take away one of your merit badges," Taylor remarked forty-five minutes later.

Will grimaced between gentle puffs of breath on the pile of smoking pocket lint and dried leaves. "The approved Firecrafter method is a bow and drill." He tilted the purpling broken glass to better catch the sun's rays. "I don't know if it's bright enough or hot enough," he muttered. "You've got wood stacked up inside if I can get this going?"

"It's all ready to go. We just have to transfer the blaze from here to there."

"The blaze…?" Will said ruefully.

They were silent, watching.

Minutes passed.

Taylor made a sharp exclamation as the pocket lint suddenly ignited. "Beautiful!"

"We're in business." Will used the glass to scoop up his tiny fire, protecting it with his hand as he stepped carefully through the broken door and put the fire to the stack of dried boards and timber Taylor had piled in the center of the lodge floor.

They stared in silent satisfaction as the flames caught.

"There's the cheese," Taylor said. "Now we just wait for mice to show up." He smiled at Will, who reached a hand behind his neck, drawing him close and kissing him.

Will was smiling, but the smile didn't reach his eyes. "You watch your back, Taylor. Understand me? Twice is all I can take."

Taylor kissed him in return, a quick, distracted press of mouths—then turned back as Will caught his arm. "You're doing it again, Will," he said softly.

"For the record, this isn't about not trusting you."

"You sure? Because that's how it feels."

Will said, "You want the truth? There's no one I'd rather have beside me in a fight than you. There's no one I trust more to watch my back."

Taylor grinned. "And your faith is well-placed, my son. I'm the best there is."

Will's hand tightened on Taylor's thinly-muscled arm. "No. Don't joke around. And don't get cocky. If something happens to you now—I don't think I'd get over it."

"That's fine," Taylor said, "because nothing is going to happen to me. And I'll tell you something else. You were afraid we couldn't do our job if we let ourselves care too much. That was one reason you didn't want to get involved. But you said it yourself this morning. We've been involved a long time—regardless of what we call ourselves: friends, lovers, partners. We're a team, Will. We always have been. We always will be."

He freed himself, catching Will's hand briefly in his own before slipping away. Frowning, Will watched him lift himself up and out through the broken window frame.

Taylor paused, balanced in the window for a moment. "And when this is over, you owe me a real vacation," he said. "We'll call it a honeymoon." The next moment he was gone, disappearing into the twilight.

Will waited, watching the fire shadow dance over the dead ranger's body.

* * * * *

They would come. Taylor had no doubt on that score. He lay in the tall grass behind the well, watching the meadow, waiting for their approach. A glance back at the lodge showed empty windows orange with firelight. Yeah, they would come, expecting to find Taylor and Will inside—maybe even sleeping.

The moon turned the waves of grass to silver. Somewhere on the other side of the building Will was lying in wait with the rifle. The thought cheered him. There was no better shot than Will. He smiled a little, thinking of Will's words before they'd separated.

Funny how he'd resented Will's overprotective streak before. Now it just felt reassuring.

If unnecessary.

The hours passed.

Taylor began to wonder if they were wrong. Maybe Bonnie and Orrin had decided to cut their losses and head for the hills.

And then he heard the rumbling in the distance—raising his head he saw lights in the distant sky. A helicopter—with search lights.

Too far away—checking the next valley over. Interesting, though. He wondered what it meant; would have liked to ask Will what he made of it.

He resisted the temptation to look for his partner. He knew he was there. He could feel him out there—hunting—just as Taylor was, and it was crucial to their survival both as a team and a couple that they prove to themselves that they could still do this. That they could still operate.

All the same, he'd have liked to know where Will was right now.

An owl hooted somewhere over on the other side of the corral: a low, raspy *who-o-o, who-o-o.*

It sounded so natural that it took Taylor a moment to recognize that call for what it was: Will checking in, letting him know where he was positioned. He grinned in the darkness, and cupped his hands, mimicking a whippoorwill—which was the only birdcall he could make that sounded halfway realistic.

As far as he knew there were no whippoorwills in the High Sierras, and he could just imagine Will shaking his head over it.

More time passed. His stomach growled. Too much longer and he'd be willing to sample the berries growing by the side of the house. He was beginning to feel his assorted aches and pains with a vengeance, his muscles stiffening up. That was liable to slow him down when the moment came.

Taylor was still mulling this over when a rifle fired, cracking the silence. He scooted out from behind the well and Orrin was striding up the meadow, firing steadily at a clump of chinquapin. He made no attempt at concealment, so he had to believe he had them cornered—which meant he already knew they weren't inside the building.

And Will wasn't firing back.

For a split second Taylor was afraid, and then he put it out of his mind, trusting Will to know what he was doing as he expected Will to trust him. He crawled forward along the outside corral, and as he did a bullet slammed into the wooden fence a few inches above his head. Bonnie—coming up from behind the lodge.

He had to give them credit; that was a smarter move than he had expected, but Orrin and Bonnie weren't taking any chances this time. Taylor dived behind a small shed. He could hear the *whup, whup, whup* of the helicopter, the searchlight skimming over the trees and fields heading down the valley—moving toward them.

Orrin was still blazing away. As Taylor watched, Will rose up out of the grass—nowhere near that chinquapin shrub.

"Drop it."

Orrin froze.

"I said drop the rifle, Orrin," Will called.

Orrin didn't move—and didn't throw the rifle away—and Taylor immediately understood. He began to look for Bonnie.

"Not going to tell you again," Will said calmly, trusting Taylor to take care of business.

Sure enough, there Bonnie was, stepping out from behind the smoke shack, drawing a bead on Will. Taylor launched himself at her, tackling her around the waist. He felt one bullet burn past his cheek—she went down firing—and he felt another bullet hit the ground next to his foot.

He slammed Bonnie against the ground—wanting it to end there, wanting to not have to punch her—and wrested the rifle from her.

She was screaming and swearing, doing her best to kick him in the balls, and then, in the distance, Taylor heard another rifle shot.

And even though he trusted Will to look after himself, for one very long second his heart forgot how to beat.

He cuffed Bonnie on the head, and she stopped fighting, sobbing with fury and frustration. Scrambling to his feet, he searched for Will, and became aware of the thrum of helicopter rotor blades drowning out everything else. Pale light bathed the yard like a spotlight. He couldn't see anything.

"Brandt?" he yelled.

"This is the California Department of Fish and Game. Put down your weapons."

Taylor stared across the blanched white yard, the tall grass whipping in the wind created by the helicopter blades.

He opened his mouth to call for Will again, but Will shouted back, "Right here, MacAllister."

"We repeat. This is California Department of Fish and Game. Put down your weapons."

Saved by the Department of Fish and Game? They were never going to live that one down. Filing that one away for future amusement, Taylor threw aside Bonnie's rifle.

"You *bastard*," Bonnie said. "I wish we'd killed you."

Taylor made a kissing sound to her, moving forward to pat her down quickly, and then stepping back.

She continued to swear a steady stream of invective as the helicopter landed, dust blowing toward them in a wave. Taylor ignored her, ignored the Fish and Game wardens piling out of the copter. He gazed across the sea of grass and spotted Orrin standing there, swaying, one arm cradling the other—and a few feet to his left, Will.

And Taylor relaxed. At last.

Feeling Taylor's gaze, Will looked across to him. He nodded. Taylor nodded back. And then Will's face broke into a grin. Taylor returned his grin.

Yeah, they were back. Back on solid ground.

Enjoy this Sneak Peek of the Next Book in the DANGEROUS GROUND Series

JOSH LANYON

CHAPTER ONE

That prickle between his shoulder blades meant he was being watched.

One hand on the mailbox, Taylor glanced around. There was a woman pushing a kid in a stroller down the long, shady street. She was moving in the opposite direction. There was a guy in a parked Chevy reading a newspaper. Old Mrs. Wills was in her garden. She was shading her eyes, staring at him.

Taylor raised his hand in greeting.

She fluttered a hand back in hello.

The guy in the Chevy turned the page of his newspaper, remaining mostly concealed behind the tall pages.

A comfortable, quiet street in a small beach community. Old houses beneath old shade trees. But it was a neighborhood in flux. Old residents dying off, new residents not staying longer than a couple of years.

Taylor pulled the mail out of his box. The usual circulars and catalogs of junk he never bought and didn't want. And a birthday card. From Will.

Taylor studied the pale green envelope for a long moment. He was aware of a tightness in his chest, a confused rush of emotions. Amusement, sure, but uppermost…a sort of…a feeling he couldn't begin to describe.

That neat, careful cursive with which Will had spelled out Taylor's name and address. Not like Will's usual hand. Not that Will's usual hand was sloppy; Taylor was the one who had to translate his hieroglyphics for the front-office staff. But there was something painstaking and self-conscious about the writing on the envelope.

There was something else in the mail slot. Taylor pulled out a slip informing him that he had a package in the side locker of the mailbox stand. He unlocked the long cabinet, and sure enough there was a rectangular parcel addressed to him. He tucked it under his arm, slammed the metal door shut, and crossed the street.

The guy in the Chevy remained well buried behind his newspaper.

Taylor cut across the patchy, threadbare lawn of his house, took the three front porch steps in one, and let himself into the house.

He locked the door behind him, looking down at the green envelope. Just the fact that Will had mailed him a birthday card. They'd be seeing each other that night—barring Will getting delayed on his current case—but Will had taken the time to pick a card and mail it. It was so…

It touched Taylor more than he wanted to admit. Of course this was a special birthday. Not one of the "0" birthdays; Taylor was thirty-two years old as of four o'clock that morning. It was special because ten weeks earlier Taylor had been shot in the chest and had nearly died.

It had been very close. The closest he'd ever come to checking out. He was still stuck on desk duty, although—thank Christ—this was the last week of that. He'd passed his fitness exam that very afternoon and Monday he'd be back in the field, partnered with Will again. Life would finally be getting back to normal. The new normal. The normal of him and Will as a…well, couple.

Partners and friends for four years, and lovers for not quite two months. Taylor was still afraid to trust it. It seemed dangerous to be this happy, like it was tempting fate. He couldn't quite forget that Will hadn't wanted this change in their relationship, that love had taken him unwilling and off guard.

He tore open the envelope.

It was the usual kind of thing. Sailboats, smooth water, and cloudless blue sky. *Happy Birthday to My Sweetheart* in sunshine yellow script.

His throat tightened. Hell. He'd never been anyone's sweetheart before. No one had ever sent him a card like this. Will had even signed the inside *Love, Will.*

There was a parcel too. A brown cardboard box. The kind of thing wine was shipped in—or good booze. The label was typed. Taylor used his pocketknife to slice through the tape sealing the box shut. Inside was a Styrofoam shell to protect the glass contents. He pried it out, and sure enough it was a bottle. A wine bottle with a yellow seal. He nearly dropped it.

There was a cobra inside the wine bottle.

Black-brown hood flared, fangs bared, the coiled cobra stared blindly through the clear rice wine.

What the fuck?

It was dead, of course. Dead and pickled. Asian snake wine was an authentic Asian beverage supposedly valuable for treating everything from rheumatism to night sweats. It was also supposed to be a natural aphrodisiac with mystical sexual properties, although what the hell was natural about a cobra in a wine bottle?

Feeling slightly queasy, Taylor set the bottle on the kitchen table.

No way had Will sent that. He searched through the box's packing materials to see if there was a card or a note. *Nada.*

Weird.

A joke maybe. Probably. He had a few friends at the Bureau of Diplomatic Security who would find this kind of thing amusing. Except it was an expensive joke. These specialty wines weren't cheap. And most of his pals at the DSS were.

He contemplated the bottle for another second or two, but he had things to get ready before Will arrived. He wanted this to be a very good weekend.

* * * * *

Taylor was not going to be happy.

Will tried to tell himself that Taylor's happiness was beside the point. Not that it didn't matter to him, but it couldn't be Will's first consideration when it came to work. Taylor was a professional. He needed to understand that this was (a) not Will's choice, (b) all part of the job, (c) no big deal, (d) all of the above.

The long red snake of taillights slithered to another halt in front of him. Will sighed and tapped the brakes, rolling to a stop. He turned up Emmylou Harris on the CD player. On the seat next to him, Riley, his German shepherd, licked his chops nervously. Riley liked traffic even less than Will did.

Traffic on the 101 was always a bitch these days, and it was especially a bitch on Friday evenings when half the Valley residents seemed to be pouring out every side street and crevice of the smoggy basin for a weekend in the mountains or at the beach.

It could take an exasperating hour just to travel from his Woodland Hills home to Ventura. Lately Taylor had been hinting that they should move in together. Will had ignored the hints.

Not that he didn't like Ventura. He did. Living that near the beach would be great, in fact. And not like he and Taylor didn't get along well. They had always got along well, even before they moved the relationship from best friends and partners to lovers.

Lovers.

Not a word Will would typically have used to describe one of his relationships. But then he wouldn't generally describe his relationships as...relationships.

The cars in front of him began to move again, brake lights flicking off, turn signals flicking on. The sea of traffic rolling forward once more.

And then…stop.

"Goddamn traffic," Will growled, and Riley flicked his ears.

Will closed his eyes, picturing his eventual arrival, savoring it, momentarily shutting out the smog and exhaust and noise of Friday evening on the 101, seeing Taylor's face in his mind: that weirdly exotic bone structure; wide green eyes that looked almost bronze; a wicked angel's full, sensual mouth; the soft, dark hair with that new—since the shooting—streak of silver.

He did not want to fight with Taylor over this thing with Bradley. He especially did not want to fight with him tonight when he had been looking forward to this evening—this weekend—all day.

They needed this time together. It had been a rough couple of weeks with Will working late most nights and Taylor increasingly frustrated with desk duty. Taylor wasn't the most patient guy in the world at the best of times. And this had not been the best of times for him.

Will had planned on a long weekend of spoiling him rotten, starting with dinner at Taylor's favorite Japanese restaurant. But now…

So did he tell Taylor the bad news up front or did he wait till Taylor was properly fed and fucked?

Emmylou sang, "I'm riding a big blue ball, I never do dream I may fall…"

"What do you think?" he asked Riley.

Riley flicked his ears and stared out the window, panting softly.

"You're no help," Will grumbled.

* * * * *

Will parked behind Taylor's silver Acura MDX in the narrow side driveway and got out of his own Toyota Land Cruiser. Evenings were damp this close to the beach. The air smelled of salt and old seaweed—corrupt yet invigorating.

He let Riley out of the passenger side of the SUV. Riley trotted down the driveway to the large, overgrown backyard, barking a warning to the neighborhood cats.

Will slid the gate shut. The house was an original Craftsman bungalow. It had been in terrible shape when Taylor bought it two years previously. Actually, it was still in terrible shape, but Taylor was renovating it, one room at a time, in his spare hours.

Will got his duffel bag from the backseat and the heavy, blue-and-gold-wrapped birthday present. He felt self-conscious about that present; he'd spent a lot of time and a fair amount of money on Taylor this year.

Hard to forget that Taylor nearly hadn't lived to see this birthday.

Speak of the devil. The side door opened, and Taylor came down the steps, an unguarded grin breaking the remote beauty of his face. There was a funny catch in Will's throat as he saw him alive and strong and smiling again.

"How was traffic?"

Will opened his mouth, but the next instant Taylor was in his arms, his mouth covering Will's in unaffected hunger. They were safe here. The cinder-block wall was high, and the bougainvillea draping over the edge of the roof neatly blocked out the view of this driveway from the street.

"Man, I missed you," Taylor said when they surfaced for air.

"You saw me this morning."

"For three minutes in front of Varga, Jabowitz, and Cooper. It's not the same."

"No," agreed Will, "it's not the same." His gaze rested on Taylor's face; his heart seemed to swell with a quiet joy. "Happy birthday."

"Thanks." Taylor's smile widened. "Hey, I got your card."

"Oh." Will was a little embarrassed about that card. *To My Sweetheart* or whatever it said. Kind of over-the-top. He'd bought it on impulse. Taylor was smiling, though, and with no sign of mockery, so maybe it was okay.

"Is that for me?" Taylor asked as Will retrieved the tote bag and parcel he'd dropped when Taylor landed in his arms.

"Nah. I'm heading over to another party after I get done here." Will shoved the blue-and-gold present into his hands. "Of course it's for you."

"Okay if I open it now?"

"You're the most impatient guy I ever met." Will was amused, though.

"Hey, I waited four years for you," Taylor threw over his shoulder, heading up the stairs into the house.

"Yeah, remind me again how you whiled away the hours in that lonely monastery?"

Taylor's chuckle drifted back.

Will heeled the side door shut and followed Taylor through the mud porch and into the kitchen.

This was one of the first rooms Taylor had renovated: a cozy breakfast nook with built-in window benches, gleaming mahogany cabinets and drawers with patinated copper fixtures, green granite counters, and gray-green slate floor. The numerous cabinets were well designed and well organized. The care and priority given the kitchen might have deceived someone into thinking cooking played a role in Taylor's life. In fact, the kitchen had been designed to please Will—the only person who had ever cooked a meal in that house.

There was a German chocolate cake on the table in the breakfast nook. Will's card was propped next to it with a couple of others: *To Our Son, To My Son, To My Brother, What is a Brother? Happy Birthday, Uncle*. Greetings from the whole tribe. To the side of these was a wine bottle-shaped science experiment gone awry.

"What the hell is that?" Will peered more closely at the pickled contents of the wine bottle. What it was, was a fucking *cobra.* The cobra stared back sightlessly at him, fangs bared.

"It's my snake. I've been waiting all day to show it to you." Taylor wiggled his eyebrows salaciously.

"Funny," said Will, glancing at him. "Where did you get it?"

"It came in the mail."

"Who sent it?"

Taylor shrugged.

"You don't know?"

"The card must have got lost."

They both studied the bottle.

"What is the liquid?"

"Rice wine."

"Is it poison?"

"It's not supposed to be. In fact, it's supposed to be a cure-all—and an aphrodisiac."

"I bet bourbon works just as well, and you don't have that nasty cobra aftertaste."

Taylor's smile was preoccupied. Will gave him a closer look.

"You don't have any idea who would have sent something like this?"

Taylor shook his head. Will laughed and threw an arm around his wide, bony shoulders.

"Spooked?"

"Nah." But Taylor's brows were drawn together as he continued to gaze at the bottle. "Weird, though, isn't it?"

"Yeah."

Taylor had some weird friends. And weirder acquaintances. He had been in the DSS longer than Will, signing on right out of college, and he'd been posted to Tokyo, Afghanistan, and briefly, Haiti. The next time he was posted overseas it would be as a regional security officer responsible for managing security operations for an embassy or for a number of diplomatic posts within an assigned area. That was one reason Will was hesitant to move in with him. Not a lot of point in setting up house when one or both of them could be stationed overseas within a year or so.

Taylor didn't see it this way, of course. Taylor's idea was they should move in together immediately and they'd deal with the threat of a future separation when—if—it happened. He'd always had a tendency to leave tomorrow to take care of itself, but getting shot had cemented his determination to live every day as though it were his last.

Will understood that. He even agreed with it, in principle, but what happened to him when Taylor was posted overseas for three-or-so years? Things weren't as simple as Taylor liked to pretend.

He glanced at Taylor's profile. He was frowning, and Will did not want him frowning on his birthday.

"Hey," he said softly. Taylor's head turned his way. "Want to open your present?"

"Sure." Taylor started to pull the gold ribbon on the parcel he was carrying. Will put his hand over his.

"Your other present," he said meaningfully, and Taylor started to laugh.

* * * * *

Will stretched out on Taylor's wide bed in the cool, dark room that looked out onto the overgrown garden with the broken birdbath and the tumbledown garden shed, and he rested his face on his hands and spread his legs.

So gorgeous. So casually, unconsciously gorgeous. Wide shoulders, strong, lithe torso, long legs. There was a tiny velvet mole above his left butt cheek and, on his right shoulder, a small griffin tattoo that he'd acquired the night before he went into the Marine Corps. Will, his brother, Grant, and their three cousins all sported those griffin tattoos on their right shoulders. Some kind of male-ritual, family-bonding thing.

Taylor had heard this from Will. He'd never met Will's family. Never met the brother or the cousins or Will's dad, who had been a sheriff in a small town in Oregon. Maybe one of these days.

He stroked a slow hand down the long, sleek line of Will's back, and Will shivered. Taylor bent his head and kissed Will right over the tiny velvet mole. Will shivered again.

Anticipation or something else?

Taylor enjoyed being fucked.

In fact, he enjoyed it so much, it made him uneasy. He'd never told Will that, but Will probably knew. Will was scrupulous about keeping the scales perfectly balanced, because they always took turns. However, though that particular evening was Taylor's turn to be fucked, Will—in honor of Taylor's birthday—offered his own taut, tanned ass up for Taylor's pleasure.

And it *was* Taylor's pleasure. Doubly so because he sensed that Will didn't enjoy being fucked nearly as much as he did, and he was humbled to receive this gift. Taylor had never let anyone shove his cock in his ass besides Will; Will was more fair-minded and had probably taken turns with his other lovers.

Taylor didn't like thinking about Will's other lovers.

He took his time preparing, squirting the exotic oil he'd purchased—ginger, jasmine, rose, black pepper, sandalwood, and ylang-ylang in a slick, silvery liquid that warmed his fingers. A sweet scent like spicy flowers.

"What's that?" Will asked, glancing over his shoulder.

"Passion oil. You'll like it."

Will resettled his chin on his folded arms. "You're into some strange shit, MacAllister."

True enough. He'd done some wild things when he was younger. Will didn't know the half of it. But in other ways he'd been very conservative. In fact, the first time he'd let Will fuck him, something had seemed to snap in his brain; made him fear he was having some kind of psychotic break. Alerted him to the fact that he probably had one or two sexual hang-ups after all. Before Will, it was unthinkable that he'd let anyone take him. Occasionally one of his lovers would ask to fuck him, and if they pushed it, that was usually Taylor's cue to end the relationship. His relationships never lasted long anyway.

Will was the exception. In every way. Though Taylor had always tried to be an inventive and skilled lover, he took special pains that everything be good for Will.

He slipped his fingers down the crevice between Will's butt cheeks, seeking the tight pink bud of his anus. *Splitting the peach*: that's what the Chinese Taoists called this. Such romantic terms for everything: *blowing the flute* and *clouds and rain* and *jade stalk*. Funny stuff but...maybe sort of nice, too.

Ever so delicately he circled Will's opening, then slipped the tip of one oily finger inside, careful and slow.

Will held very still, goose bumps rising over his smooth, tanned skin.

Taylor pushed inside, closing his eyes at the dark-felt grip around his finger. His heart pounded hard, his own cock lifted—*arisen*, *angry*, those old Chinese would have said, but Taylor was anything but angry. Happy, excited...he stroked and pressed...satiny inside and satiny out.

"Does that feel good?" he murmured.

"Sure." Will sounded a little winded.

Taylor silently cued Will to move onto his knees; even here they could communicate deftly without words. He guided his cock, already pearling and damp, and pushed slowly, inch by inch, into Will. "Are you —"

"Go," Will jerked out. "Do it."

Was Will loving it or just wanting it over with? Taylor was never quite sure, but he couldn't stop himself at this point. Will was pushing back against him, rocking into him. Taylor thrust back, and they settled into a quick, efficient rhythm.

Oh yes. More. More of this. Harder. Deeper. Faster. Taylor's eyes shut tight. Just feeling, feeling that gorgeous drag on the thick, pulsing shaft of his cock, feeling the heat and snug darkness, feeling everything.

Will grunted as Taylor changed angle, tried to hit the sweet spot just right.

"Good, Will?" gasped Taylor.

"Yeah. Good."

So good—but it was good all the ways they did it. And they had done it nearly every conceivable way. At least all the ways that Taylor figured wouldn't shock or dismay Will. Very much a meat-and-potatoes man, Will.

Will's harsh breaths were coming in counterpoint to his own. The rich, rolling sweetness tingled through Taylor, and he cried out as Will's body seemed to spasm around his own and he began to come in hard, hot jets *clouds and rain, firing the cannon, surrender, and die…*

ABOUT THE AUTHOR

Author of over sixty titles of classic Male/Male fiction featuring twisty mystery, kickass adventure, and unapologetic man-on-man romance, JOSH LANYON'S work has been translated into twelve languages. Her FBI thriller *Fair Game* was the first Male/Male title to be published by Harlequin Mondadori, then the largest romance publisher in Italy. *Stranger on the Shore* (Harper Collins Italia) was the first M/M title to be published in print. In 2016 *Fatal Shadows* placed #5 in Japan's annual Boy Love novel list (the first and only title by a foreign author to place on the list). The Adrien English series was awarded the All Time Favorite Couple by the Goodreads M/M Romance Group. In 2019, *Fatal Shadows* became the first LGBTQ mobile game created by Moments: Choose Your Story.

She is an Eppie Award winner, a four-time Lambda Literary Award finalist (twice for Gay Mystery), An Edgar nominee, and the first ever recipient of the Goodreads All Time Favorite M/M Author award.

Josh is married and lives in Southern California.

Find other Josh Lanyon titles at www.joshlanyon.com, and follow Josh on Twitter, Facebook, Goodreads, Instagram and Tumblr.

For extras and exclusives, join Josh on Patreon.

ALSO BY JOSH LANYON

NOVELS

The ADRIEN ENGLISH Mysteries

Fatal Shadows • A Dangerous Thing • The Hell You Say
Death of a Pirate King • The Dark Tide
So This is Christmas • Stranger Things Have Happened

The HOLMES & MORIARITY Mysteries

Somebody Killed His Editor • All She Wrote
The Boy with the Painful Tattoo • In Other Words...Murder

The ALL'S FAIR Series

Fair Game • Fair Play • Fair Chance

The ART OF MURDER Series

The Mermaid Murders •The Monet Murders
The Magician Murders • The Monuments Men Murders

The SECRETS AND SCRABBLE Series

Murder at Pirate's Cove

OTHER NOVELS

The Ghost Wore Yellow Socks
Mexican Heat (with Laura Baumbach)
Strange Fortune • Come Unto These Yellow Sands
This Rough Magic • Stranger on the Shore • Winter Kill
Murder in Pastel • Jefferson Blythe, Esquire
The Curse of the Blue Scarab • Murder Takes the High Road
Séance on a Summer's Night
The Ghost Had an Early Check-Out

NOVELLAS

The DANGEROUS GROUND Series

Dangerous Ground • Old Poison • Blood Heat
Dead Run • Kick Start • Blind Side

The I SPY Series

I Spy Something Bloody • I Spy Something Wicked
I Spy Something Christmas

The IN A DARK WOOD Series

In a Dark Wood • The Parting Glass

The DARK HORSE Series

The Dark Horse • The White Knight

The DOYLE & SPAIN Series

Snowball in Hell

The HAUNTED HEART Series

Haunted Heart Winter

The XOXO FILES Series

Mummie Dearest

OTHER NOVELLAS

Cards on the Table • The Dark Farewell •The Darkling Thrush
The Dickens with Love • Don't Look Back • A Ghost of a Chance
Lovers and Other Strangers • Out of the Blue
A Vintage Affair • Lone Star (in Men Under the Mistletoe)
Green Glass Beads (in Irregulars) • Blood Red Butterfly
Everything I Know • Baby, It's Cold • A Case of Christmas
Murder Between the Pages • Slay Ride

SHORT STORIES

A Limited Engagement • The French Have a Word for It
In Sunshine or In Shadow • Until We Meet Once More
Icecapade (in His for the Holidays) • Perfect Day
Heart Trouble • In Plain Sight • Wedding Favors
Wizard's Moon • Fade to Black • Night Watch
Plenty of Fish • The Boy Next Door
Halloween is Murder

COLLECTIONS

Stories (Vol. 1) • Sweet Spot (the Petit Morts)
Merry Christmas, Darling (Holiday Codas)
Christmas Waltz (Holiday Codas 2)
I Spy...Three Novellas
Point Blank (Five Dangerous Ground Novellas)
Dark Horse, White Knight (Two Novellas)
The Adrien English Mysteries
The Adrien English Mysteries 2

Made in the USA
Las Vegas, NV
27 November 2021

35404113R00075